LINGER

Edward Fallon

#6

Mark
of the
Beast

BRAUN HAUS MEDIA, LLC

The publisher wishes to acknowledge and thank
Allan Leverone
for his contribution to this work

Other books in the *Linger* series
available for purchase now

LINGER 6

Mark of the Beast

PART ONE

"It is easier to build strong children than to repair broken men."
~Frederick Douglass

1

The needle hurt when the man jabbed it into her wrist.

It hurt a lot.

But she didn't cry. Not right away at least.

Between her utter surprise at the man's sudden arrival and the additional shock of discovering that he would soon be working on *her*—whatever that meant—it had somehow never occurred to her overstressed brain to trigger the crying reflex.

But it kicked in soon enough.

Because the man was as big as a beast. And ugly. And he carried himself with the grim, focused ferocity of a monster straight out of her worst nightmares.

And the girl knew a little bit about nightmares.

The crying started once the man *really* got down to work. Bent over her upturned arm like a surgeon summoned from hell, all silent intimidation and barely controlled rage, stabbing her soft skin with the needle again and again and again, and the girl just couldn't help herself.

She began to sob.

"Shut up," the man said after a couple of minutes.

He never stopped working, barely even glancing up from the girl's wrist. But those two simple syllables conveyed more evil intent than any amount of threatening would have.

And she tried to stop crying. She really tried. The girl wasn't stupid, and any idiot could have seen this intruder wasn't someone to be taken lightly.

For a while, she even succeeded. She locked away the pain and the fear and the confusion in the hidden corner of her brain where she typically relegated her mother's unrelenting criticism and ridicule, from which the girl got a break only during those times when she was being utterly ignored.

She called that hidden corner of her brain "the storage locker." No one knew of its existence but her. She had never spoken of it, not even to her friends. She needed that storage locker desperately, and her biggest fear—until today, at least—was that talking about her special locker, quantifying it and making it real, would cause it to disappear like a needle popping a bubble.

The thought of a needle brought the girl back to the present, to her current terrifying reality, and with her return came the tears. Again. Small sobs, accompanied by a couple of tracks down her cheeks that tickled her skin but that she was too afraid to wipe away with her free hand.

If she stayed perfectly still, maybe the man wouldn't notice the tears. Wouldn't become angry with her and cause her even more pain.

Eventually he did notice, of course, and it became clear to the girl that her sniffles and sobs were beginning to get under his skin.

No pun intended.

The girl tried to occupy herself by peering at the semicircle of chairs arranged around the two of them like intimate theater seating, as if a dozen or so people had been invited to witness some kind of bizarre performance art.

But doing so only worsened her building terror. The faces staring back at her were uniform in their blankness. Pale, drawn ovals with uncomprehending eyes and slack expressions. They looked like zombies out of a scary movie.

Even Billy. The girl tried to catch his eyes, wanted to convey some kind of reassurance to him, but her attempt failed miserably. Billy's eyes were every bit as vacant as the other children's.

She looked next at Mr. LeBlanc—Peter—who stood to one side, near the ring of children. And what she saw on his face only intensified her own anxiety. Normally strong and competent, he was wide-eyed. Obviously frightened. Unsure of what to do.

When she caught his gaze, his trembling attempt at a smile only deepened her dread, conveying everything she needed to know.

This was bad.

It was really bad.

And it would only get worse.

She wanted to tell Peter that she was okay, for now at least, that the physical pain was manageable even though the terror was crippling. But there was no way to do this without drawing the ire of the big, beastly man. And besides, the tears had started up again, this time in earnest. They sprang from her eyes as if two faucets had been abruptly opened full-force.

This time, no amount of willpower could hold them back.

This time, the girl doubted they would ever stop.

2

Kate Messenger didn't realize the significance of the news report the first time it ran.

The TV was on, tuned to Headline News, but neither she nor Weston had been paying much attention to it. They had turned the volume down, so that it was almost but not quite muted, relegating it to little more than background noise as the rain fell and the wind howled outside their drafty motel room.

Christopher was the one who noticed and drew their attention to the report. Christopher, the boy who could neither see nor speak out loud about what was on the TV. But that didn't mean he couldn't communicate.

Kate and Weston were bickering, disagreeing about something stupid—where to go for dinner, as if it really mattered—when Chris interrupted them with a single word that flashed into Kate's mind unbidden:

Brunswick.

She stopped speaking mid-sentence, her point immediately forgotten, and turned toward the boy. He'd been sitting on one of the double beds for much of the afternoon, rocking gently, his face tilted toward the ceiling.

"Excuse me?" It was all she could think of to say.

The news report. On TV. It's about a murder and it's for us.

"Which murder? What are you talking about?"

Kate turned back toward Weston, who shook his head and spread his hands. She picked up the remote and aimed it toward the screen, raising the volume on a story about an octogenarian in Nebraska who had been in a coma for nearly three decades, but had awoken without warning yesterday, seemingly in perfect health, thinking the year was 1987. His long-suffering wife was still by his side, praising the power of prayer and modern medicine.

"There's no murder here," Kate said.

You missed it.

Chris sounded reproachful, even though his voice existed only in her head.

It was the previous report and you missed it. You needed to see that story. We all needed to see it.

"We still can," Weston said. "That station runs on a loop. It'll play again, within the hour. All we have to do is wait."

So they did.

The silver-haired anchor gazed into the camera, his telegenic face arranged in a mask of grim, ruggedly handsome sincerity. "A disturbing murder in central Maine has local authorities baffled."

A photograph of a young man, perhaps twenty-five years of age, with a thick mane of brown hair and a sheepish smile, appeared behind the anchor's left shoulder as he continued.

"Peter LeBlanc was found murdered early yesterday morning just outside the grounds of a special needs group home in Brunswick where he had worked as a counselor for the past three years. Authorities are being tight-lipped about the case, but an anonymous source close to the investigation claims that the victim's tongue was cut out in what has all the appearances of ritual, cult-like activity. We take you now to Jeanie Gerard, live on the scene in Brunswick, Maine. Jeanie?"

The man's face vanished from the screen and was replaced by a younger, blonde female, with an equally telegenic face, dressed in a conservative grey blazer covering a plain white blouse that revealed just a hint of cleavage. She stood in front of a rambling old brick building that resembled an ancient prison, or perhaps a B-movie insane asylum. A black wrought-iron fence surrounded the property, and the front gate was closed, the area cordoned off by yellow police tape.

"That's right, Dan. The victim was found just outside the parking lot of the Maine Home for Children with Special Needs, but police in this quiet northern Maine city aren't revealing much so far. When I asked Chief Rich Berman to confirm or deny our report that the murdered man's tongue had been removed, he refused any comment. None of our sources would speculate on a potential motive for the killing, but the ritualistic aspect of the brutal crime has neighbors on edge.

"Police would not say whether they think Peter LeBlanc's employment here is in any way related to his murder, but residents we spoke to believe the location of his body cannot possibly be coincidental."

The scene cut to a pre-taped interview. The pretty blonde held a microphone in front of a man dressed in an unbuttoned flannel shirt over a New England Patriots t-shirt.

He shook his head and said, "Why anyone would want to murder and disfigure a guy who works with the less fortunate I'll never understand, but it seems like there has to be a connection. Why kill him in plain sight of these poor kids?"

He took one step back and pointed through the fence at a parking lot inside. "The guy's car is in there, and yet his body is discovered out here. Doesn't make any sense, right? Why was he even outside the gate when his car is all the way back there?"

The scene cut back to the blonde and she said, "It seems clear this is more than just your typical murder, Dan. Other people we spoke to, who chose not to appear on camera, told us that this crime drives home just how isolated Brunswick is as a community. 'There are millions of acres of forest out there,' one woman told me. 'Who knows how many weird cults are in operation, or what they might be planning to do next?'

"This murder has affected not just one person or even one family, Dan, but rather an entire city. We'll be following the story closely over the coming days, and will file additional reports as more details become available. This is Jeanie Gerard, live in Brunswick, Maine."

The silver-haired anchor reappeared on screen and shook his head gravely. "Frightening story, Jeanie, thank you."

Kate thumbed the "Mute" button and for a moment no one spoke, and then Christopher's voice filled her head again.

We need to go to Brunswick.

She looked at Weston, only to find him staring back at her unblinkingly. He had probably been watching her for most of the report.

He said, "Know anything about Maine?"

"I'm told they have the world's best lobster."

"Ever been there?"

"Nope."

"Me neither."

"When are we leaving?"

"First thing in the morning."

3

The security guard crouched motionless over the dead woman's body, shining his flashlight on her, drinking in the sight of the corpse sprawled lifelessly between two dumpsters.

He didn't secure the scene.

Didn't get on his mall-issued walkie-talkie and radio for help.

Didn't do anything.

He simply stared at the victim. Then he stood and moved closer. Leaned down. Placed his flashlight on the ground so that its beam splashed the victim's face. Reached out and closed the dead woman's startled, empty eyes.

He then placed his hand inside her mouth and grasped her tongue. Pulled until it was fully—and obscenely—extended. He held the tongue with his left hand as he reached for his belt with his right and lifted out a utility knife. His inner right wrist sported what looked like a crude jailhouse tattoo: a black circle with a dot in the center, like the mark of a bulls-eye.

He flicked the utility knife open, and as he lowered it toward the woman's tongue—

Kate's eyes flew open and she gasped, sweat dripping from her hairline and down her face. She felt her heart racing, felt her breath coming in gasps, as though she had just run a marathon.

Weston glanced at her across the front seat of their ancient Rambler station wagon, his eyebrows knitted together. "Nightmare?"

Kate didn't quite trust herself to speak. She hated showing weakness, ever and to anyone, but especially to Weston. Even now, after months spent traveling the country in the company of this man, bound together by the bonds of shared tragedy, she detested revealing more of herself than was absolutely necessary. And allowing Noah Weston to hear a quaver in her voice was absolutely *not* necessary.

So she nodded instead.

His eyes narrowed and he continued to stare, and annoyance overcame her reluctance to speak.

"Would you please return your attention to the road before we become one with a tree?"

He frowned and turned forward, shaking his head slightly.

Kate calmed herself. "I hadn't even realized I was tired before I dozed off. I guess the hum of the highway under the tires and the sun beating through the window must have lulled me to sleep."

"You know, there's nothing wrong in admitting you had a bad dream, or in talking about it. It might make you feel better."

"I'm fine," she said sourly.

Weston refused to let it go. "It doesn't mean there's anything wrong with you. Hell, given our situation, there'd probably be something wrong if you *didn't* have a nightmare every now and then. I've certainly had my share."

"I said I'm *fine*. Can you please drop it?" The words came out sharper than intended, but Kate couldn't bring herself to back off. She glared at him, her eyes boring holes in the side of his head.

He refused to acknowledge the death stare but she knew he could see her.

"No problem," he said. "It's just that I understand what you're going through. We both do." He indicated the back seat with a nod of his head.

Kate turned to look at Christopher. The boy was sitting quietly, head back. Were it not for the slight but ceaseless movement as he rocked back and forth, she would have thought he was dozing, too.

But he wasn't asleep. He was just... elsewhere.

In a way she was glad he was awake. She knew from personal experience that he, too, suffered from nightmares, but it was impossible to know just how disturbing his dreams were or how regularly they occurred.

And Weston was right about one thing. It would be understandable if he had them every night. Because Kate Messenger might have seen her share of tragedy, but that little boy had seen more.

Much more.

Her eyes were beginning to droop again when a big green sign flashed past on the side of Interstate 95, indicating BRUNSWICK, NEXT THREE EXITS.

A California girl, born and raised, Kate Messenger had never visited Maine. Had never wanted to, and had never planned to until three nights ago, when Chris made it clear it should be their next destination.

The fact that she hadn't even raised an eyebrow when the boy's melodic voice appeared inside her head and brought the news report to her attention, was an indication of how much her life had changed since meeting him.

For Christopher, telepathy was his only method of verbal communication. As a victim of the Beast, his tongue had been savagely cut out, as had the tongues of most of the other young residents of the group home in which he had been living.

With one exception, the rest of the children had died in that attack—as had Christopher.

But Christopher was different.

Christopher had come back.

And now—when he chose to and when he was not lost in the haze inside his own head—he communicated by projecting his thoughts into Kate and Weston's minds. Several months ago, this bizarre ability had caused Kate to question her sanity.

Now she barely noticed.

But as they drove toward Brunswick, Christopher said nothing. Neither Kate nor Weston had any idea where he went when he checked out, or for how long he would be gone.

"Which exit should we take?" she asked.

Weston shrugged. "Good question. I was hoping our little friend would—"

Take the second exit.

Kate looked again into the back seat. Christopher sat as he had before, rocking back and forth, his sightless eyes fixed on a spot roughly approximating the dome of the Rambler's interior light.

But something had changed.

He was back.

Or was he?

"The second exit it is," Weston said. He had begun to slow in anticipation of turning onto the first off-ramp, and now he accelerated back to highway speed.

"Care to share why the second exit and not the first or the third?" Kate asked over her shoulder.

But no answer was forthcoming. Chris may or may not have heard her. There was no way to know for sure. This was the hardest part of traveling with such a special child.

For a woman whose entire existence—professionally and personally—had long been predicated on maintaining control, the boy's unpredictable disappearances were among the most frustrating things imaginable.

She sighed deeply and faced forward.

The second Brunswick exit was approaching in the distance. They would take the turnoff and see what happened next.

4

When they heard nothing further from Chris, Kate said to Weston, "Since we don't have any particular plan, what do you think about stopping for some chow?"

"I could eat," Weston said. "I don't suppose you have any suggestions *where*?"

"Seeing as how I've never been here before, I think you know the answer to that. Maybe we can try some of that world-famous lobster."

They drove in silence, the off-ramp merging onto another two-lane highway that would take them, presumably, into Brunswick proper.

"So what do you think?" Kate asked.

"About what? Lobster?"

"No. The odds our guy is still here?"

"I thought we were discussing lunch?"

"We were. Now we're discussing the Beast."

Weston shook his head. "Probably pretty low. Even if he's the one behind this guy LeBlanc's murder."

"It's him."

"Could be a copycat. Don't forget those two whack jobs in Florida."

"That was different. LeBlanc's missing tongue and the location of the murder have the Beast written all over it. We're talking about a *group home*, for Christ's sake. That's too close to what happened to Chris to be a copycat *or* coincidental." She paused for a moment. "But it's been three days, so I do agree he's probably long gone by now."

I'm not so sure about that.

Kate raised her eyebrows involuntarily, jarred by Chris's sudden entrance into the conversation.

"You think he's still here?" She tried to keep the skepticism out of her voice but mostly failed.

I don't know. It doesn't make sense for him to stay, but..."

His "voice" trailed off and after a couple of seconds, Weston prompted, "But?"

Something doesn't feel right. He might still be around.

A jolt of excitement surged through Kate, and she had to force herself to tamp it down. Christopher's insights were often right on the money, but he wasn't infallible, and this could well be one of those times.

Maybe he was misreading whatever psychic energy the Beast had left behind on his way out of town. Maybe he was letting wishful thinking get in the way of his own objectivity.

Or maybe he was just tired.

Chris's comment had raised questions in her mind, a lot of them, but asking him about it would be pointless. If he could be more specific, he would.

She settled for saying, "You'll let us know if anything becomes clear."

Of course.

She glanced across the front seat at Weston, who returned her gaze without speaking.

"Whether he's moved on or not," she said, "at least we know he *was* here. And this may be our best opportunity to pick up his trail again."

Weston nodded. "Let's hope you're right."

It had been weeks since the Beast had been on their radar, and after some false starts and several dead ends as they zig-zagged across the country, Kate and Weston had grown more and more frustrated, wondering if he'd gone to ground. In some ways his silence had been more disturbing than his previous activities, and while Kate was horrified by this most recent act of butchery, she also relished the thought that they might once again have caught up with the monster.

The highway had dumped them onto more typical surface

streets, which were relatively busy with mid-afternoon traffic but still moving at a reasonable pace. Kate squinted against the sunshine streaming in through the side window. Up ahead, a young girl faced the oncoming traffic on the right side of the road, thumb stuck out in search of a ride.

She was long-legged, wearing jeans shorts so small they would have made Daisy Duke blush. A crop top revealed most of a tanned midriff. Her blonde hair had been pulled into a ponytail that trailed out the back of a *Portland Sea Dogs* baseball cap. She walked slowly backward with the bored indifference of someone to whom thumbing a ride was not a novel experience.

Kate shook her head. Even here in the middle of nowhere—hell, *especially* here in the middle of nowhere—a young girl hitchhiking by herself was a bad idea.

Theoretically speaking, Kate agreed wholeheartedly with the concept that any woman should be able to dress however she wanted and feel perfectly safe. Even while hitchhiking. But as a practical matter, and as a longtime police officer, Kate knew the opposite was often true. Having *the right* to do something safely was not the same as actually having *the ability* to.

Kate had investigated more crimes than she could count that had hammered that particular point home, and pursed her lips in disapproval as she stared out the windshield at the girl.

When the Rambler swept past the outstretched thumb, Kate realized the hitchhiker was young. Maybe fifteen. Or not much older.

Weston glanced disinterestedly in the girl's direction, and Kate spread her hands. "Well?"

"What? Did you spot a restaurant?"

"No, I didn't spot a restaurant. The girl, Noah. The girl."

"What about her?"

"Aren't you gonna stop?"

Weston half-shrugged and shook his head. "Why would I stop?"

He was clearly mystified, and Kate stuck her tongue against the roof of her mouth. She was tired and hungry and annoyed, the annoyance rapidly morphing into genuine anger. "Didn't you notice how young she is?"

"Not really, why?"

"She's just a kid, for godsakes. She shouldn't be hitchhiking by herself—shouldn't be hitchhiking at all—and especially not now, given what happened in this town a few days ago."

"We're not here to save the world, Kate. Every minute we waste, we fall a minute farther behind the Beast."

Kate jabbed a finger at him. "Pull over and pick her up. We're gonna make sure she's safe before we do anything else."

"Look," Weston said heatedly, "I appreciate your concern for humanity, but our first priority is—"

Stop arguing. Please.

Weston frowned. "We aren't arguing, Chris. We're having a discuss—"

Pick her up. You have to pick her up. Do it now.

"But why?"

I don't know. Just do it.

There was an urgency to the boy's tone that surprised Kate, and she knew Weston would no more ignore his command than he would voluntarily drive the Rambler into oncoming traffic.

Neither would *she* when it came down to it.

Weston raised his eyebrows and cocked his head to the side in a slight expression of his own annoyance, but he didn't say another word, and immediately began slowing. By now they were a good distance away, so he waited for a break in traffic and flipped a U, then headed in the opposite direction until they saw the girl still thumbing on the other side of the road. Weston made another U-turn and eased to a stop about six feet in front of her.

Kate cranked down her window and flashed what she hoped was a reassuring smile, but the girl snapped her gum and didn't return it.

She studied them a moment, then trudged to the car, and Kate saw immediately that she would have to revise her original estimate in regard to age. There was no way this girl was fifteen. Thirteen was probably more accurate, and even that guess might be generous.

But that wasn't what really drew Kate's attention.

In fact, all thoughts of age were immediately abandoned when the girl reached out and pulled open the Rambler's rear door, and Kate saw her right wrist. The skin was smooth and the wrist thin—coltish like the girl's legs—and sported a healthy midsummer tan.

And it was tattooed.

A crude circle with a single dot in the middle.

5

Chris scooted over and let the girl slide in.

"Thanks for the ride," she said noncommittally, and met Kate's gaze for just a moment before turning to look out the window.

Kate glanced at Weston. The surprise and confusion on his face were enough to tell her that he had seen the tattoo as well. She suspected she'd find that same expression on her own face if she were to look into a mirror right now.

"No problem," she said after a short hesitation. "Where are you headed?"

The girl ignored the question. She had turned in her seat and was staring head-on at Christopher. She made no attempt to hide her interest in him, and her gaze locked onto the milky caul covering his eyes.

Kate had long since gotten used to the curiosity people tended to exhibit upon first seeing Chris, but such direct attention was rare, especially from another child. Kids—and many adults—tended to avert their eyes from him, stealing furtive glances when they thought they weren't being observed, as if fearful that his affliction might be contagious.

Not this girl. Kate watched as her eyes wandered over Christopher's face.

"He's blind," she said without any trace of self-consciousness.

Weston eased back onto the highway and glanced at her in his rearview mirror. "Yes. And he can't speak, either."

"Why not?"

"He's... been through a lot."

The whole exchange was jarring, entirely unexpected, and Kate decided it was time to change the subject. "You didn't answer my question. Where do you want us to take you?"

The girl finally turned away from Chris. "Anywhere."

Kate couldn't help but shoot Weston a second glance. Her unease deepened as she took a closer look at the girl. Her hair was clumped and matted. Her dirty clothing looked as though it had been slept in at least a night, if not more.

"Anywhere, huh?" Kate was careful to keep her voice light and non-threatening. "Then I guess there's no danger we'll get lost on the way."

The corner of the girl's lips may have twitched slightly, but otherwise she offered no response.

"What's your name, sweetheart?"

The girl sat quietly for a moment and Kate thought she might ignore the question. Then she said, "Dani."

"Hi, Dani, I'm Kate. Noah's driving and your seatmate is Christopher."

The girl turned toward Chris and said, "It's nice to meet you, Christopher. I know you can't answer, but that's okay. You don't have to, I don't mind."

Chris nodded. The ease with which Dani seemed to be relating to him was astounding.

With her mind, Kate asked Chris, *What's going on here?*

The answer was instantaneous, almost as if he had been waiting for the question. *She's involved. I can feel it. That's why I told Noah to pick her up.*

Involved how?

I don't know. I can't decipher it. There's too much going on with her.

She has the tattoo, Chris.

Yes, I know.

What does it mean?

I... I'm not sure.

Frustration threatened to overwhelm Kate. Who was this girl, and how was she related to the Beast? And why was she relating to Christopher so easily when most children treated him like a boy with leprosy?

"What's your last name, Dani?"

The girl hesitated again and then said, "Melanson."

Before Kate could say anything else, Weston cut in, "You look like you might be hungry, and I'm starving. We were all on our way to get something to eat. Would you like to join us?"

The girl licked her lips in an unconscious gesture. It was clear she was hungry, and Kate pressed the issue a little harder. "Are you from around here? Maybe you could help us pick out a good restaurant. None of us have ever been to Maine before, and we'd love to try some fresh lobster."

Again the girl hesitated before speaking, and again Kate thought she might not answer. But then, as before, she did.

"The Lobster Claw," she said quietly. Almost too quietly to be heard.

But Kate heard it. She said, "Sounds perfect. Do you know how to get there from here?"

The girl locked eyes with Kate for a moment before lifting up in the seat, stretching to look out the front window. It was a short glance, no more than a second, but plenty of time for Kate to read the expression in her eyes.

She was afraid.

She was trying very hard not to show it, but she was afraid.

The show of fear was brief and then the mask of carefully controlled composure returned to her face. "Take your next left, the one at the light."

Weston flicked on his blinker and began slowing for the red light. Before the car could come to a complete stop the light turned green and he accelerated through the turn onto a street that looked very similar to the last. Kate knew he was hanging on her every word and had been since spotting the tattoo.

Kate had turned sideways in her seat so she could observe their young passenger, and as Dani concentrated on the view out the windshield, Kate took advantage of the chance to more closely examine the girl's tattoo.

It was clearly an amateur job, probably a rush job as well. The lines of the circle were crudely drawn, not smooth and not even fully circular. And the tattoo appeared fresh. Recent. Maybe very recent. The skin surrounding the area was still pink and tender, not yet fully recovered from the trauma of the needle.

Equally strange was the fact that as far as Kate could see, the girl didn't have a single tattoo anywhere else on her body, and she was showing plenty of skin. And how many parents would allow a child so young to get a tattoo anyway?

It seemed clear from Dani's appearance that she was a runaway, a situation that represented the first real act of rebellion for many teens. Maybe the tattoo had been an extension of that rebellion. It wouldn't be the first time Kate had seen a similar stunt. There was no way to know without more information.

Dani was definitely from this area, or at least familiar with the city of Brunswick. She issued a right turn and then a left, seemingly beginning to relax in the company of the two adults in the front seat. In a matter of minutes, a wooden sign cut into the shape of a giant lobster claw loomed over the side of the road, and Kate knew they had arrived.

The restaurant was small, a perfectly square, somewhat ramshackle, wood-framed box that she guessed couldn't seat more than a couple dozen diners. It was located between a do-it-yourself car wash and a stove shop, and the lack of vehicles parked in the lot suggested getting a table wouldn't present a problem.

"Are you sure this is the right place?" Kate asked, eyeing the structure skeptically.

Dani nodded and Weston drove into the lot.

They had finally arrived in Brunswick after two and a half days on the road. And if the tattoo on Dani's wrist was any indication, they had driven right into the middle of something big.

The question was, what?

6

Weston parked the Rambler in a shaded spot. Kate climbed out, crossed around the front of the car and stood next to Weston, waiting for Christopher to exit the back seat. His ability to get around despite his blindness was uncanny, but a parking lot meant drivers who may not be paying attention, and she had every intention of helping him into the restaurant despite the protests she knew would follow.

The rear door opened and Chris slid out, followed immediately by Dani. The girl took his hand gently and began leading him toward the entrance as Kate and Weston watched, still standing beside the car, too surprised to move.

At the doorway, Dani turned and said, "Aren't you coming?"

"Curiouser and curiouser," Kate mumbled as they followed the children into the restaurant.

Dani dug into her meal with gusto.

She clearly hadn't eaten in some time, further confirming Kate's suspicion she was probably a runaway. Kate shared a glance with Weston and an unspoken agreement to allow Dani to eat her fill before they began trying to mine her for information.

But the fact remained that someone, likely someone right here in Brunswick, was missing this girl or would be soon, and Kate and Weston's time with her would be limited. If she wouldn't admit to having a family here, or refused to reveal her address, the authorities would have to handle her situation.

But such measures could wait. Kate had no intention of giving up access to this mysterious child until she could extract as much information as possible.

For now, it was easy to convince herself to give Dani a little breathing room because the food was delicious. The lobster was fresh and juicy, the butter hot, and the coffee rich and flavorful. The Lobster Claw might have been a tiny dive, but it was hard to imagine the finest restaurant in Brunswick serving anything better.

As she ate, Kate ran the scene in the parking lot through her mind over and over. The way the girl had taken Christopher's hand and helped him, like it was the most natural thing in the world. It was almost as if she was used to special needs kids.

But Dani was clearly not special needs herself. Despite her reluctance to answer questions, or to say much of anything beyond the directions necessary to get them here, there was nothing to indicate she was anything more than a typical young girl.

A typical teen who had been through some sort of recent trauma.

Kate and Weston had finished their meal and were both into their second cups of coffee before their new friend began to show any signs of slowing her eating pace.

Christopher had finished long ago, and Kate and Weston made small talk—whether they should fill the Rambler's gas tank after lunch, checking *Yelp* listings for a decent but cheap motel—while waiting for the right moment to attempt a meaningful conversation with the girl.

While they waited for Dani to finish eating, Kate tried again with Christopher. *Are you getting anything? Any clearer on this girl's connection to the Beast?*

No response.

He either could not or would not answer.

Finally Dani placed her knife and fork neatly on the ravaged dinner plate and looked up. She was careful to make eye contact with both of them, starting with Kate and moving to Weston, and then she said, "Thank you."

Kate caught Weston's eye and nodded almost imperceptibly toward the girl, silently asking him to take the lead in the conversation that was to follow. She was well aware of her own tendency toward bluntness—Weston had once called her "rude and stubborn"—and while she felt he might have overstated things just a bit, she also realized a more subtle touch might lead to better results, particularly with someone so young.

Plus, she wanted to devote her full attention to analyzing Dani's mannerisms as she talked. What a person said was often less significant than how it was said.

Weston nodded in response and sat for a moment. Then he said, "You know what I could use right now?"

Nobody answered, but Dani lifted her face to look at him, eyebrows raised.

"I could really use a piece of pie, and maybe some ice cream. Who wants to join me?"

Kate seriously doubted Weston could still be hungry after all they had eaten, but given how vigorously Dani had attacked her plate, she guessed his question stood as good a chance as any of eliciting a positive response, which was obviously what he was going for.

Unless, of course, Dani hated pie.

He caught the girl's eye, smiling broadly, and in that moment, Kate saw a glimpse of the kind of father Noah Weston must have once been to his own daughters. Grief and circumstances had hardened the man, but seeing him interact with this child was simultaneously inspiring and sad.

And it worked. Dani's eyes sparkled and an actual smile crossed her face for the first time. It was hesitant, and it disappeared almost immediately, but it was there. And while it was there it lit up her face and amply illustrated what a beautiful young woman Dani Melanson would be in just a few years time.

She said, "I like pie."

"And ice cream?"

"Of course!"

He grinned. "Then let's get some."

They called the waitress over and placed the dessert order—Kate settled for a third cup of coffee—and when the woman walked away, Weston said, "I'm impressed with how easily you got us to the Lobster Claw, Dani. And the meal was amazing. Thank you for the recommendation."

She shrugged, embarrassed by the attention, and said, "Brunswick's not that big."

"Still, you definitely know the town, and we really appreciate you leading us to the best place around. I don't know what we would have done if we hadn't met up with you. Personally, I think you saved us from a terrible fate: burned hamburgers and greasy fries."

Weston was being uncharacteristically charming. Kate had seen this side of him before, on rare occasions, and it always came as a surprise.

This time, she watched in amusement as Dani actually laughed at Weston's remark. Kate would have approached the situation from a different angle, diving right in with a question about the wrist tattoo, but Weston seemed to know what he was doing. Dani was clearly much more at ease than she had been before.

It was a good start.

When dessert arrived, Weston smiled in amusement as Dani dug into her pie with the same enthusiasm as she had attacked her lobster a few minutes ago.

"So tell me," he said as she lifted a forkful into her mouth and began chewing. "Where can we take you when we leave here? You look like you've been on a bit of an adventure, and someone must be worried about you."

The words were no sooner out of his mouth than the girl stiffened. She swallowed heavily and placed her fork next to the plate, pie forgotten. Her eyes grew wide and her hands started to tremble.

"I'm not going back there by myself," she said. "You can't make me go back, I won't do it."

"Easy," Weston told her, lifting his hands in a conciliatory gesture. "We're not here to hurt you, and we won't make you do anything that will put you in danger. That's the first thing you need to understand."

He pushed his plate to the side and bent forward, lowering his face to meet the frightened girl's eyes with his own.

"Do you understand that? We take care of Christopher and make sure nothing bad happens to him. We're pretty good at it, too. I promise you, we will not allow anything to happen to you while you're with us."

She nodded uncertainly, the motion quick and abbreviated. Kate thought she looked exactly like a scared rabbit. She didn't lift her eyes but she didn't look away from Weston, either.

Kate was thankful that the Lobster Claw was nearly empty, because while Dani wasn't making a scene, her fear was plain to see and if anyone happened to notice, they might be dealing with a visit from the Brunswick Police Department very soon.

"Now, in order for us to protect you," Weston continued gently, "we have to know what's gotten you so frightened. That makes sense, right?"

Another quick nod.

"Okay. Why were you hitchhiking today? It seems like you were running away from something. What would that be?"

She lifted her head. She looked from Weston to Kate, even glanced briefly at Christopher, who was rocking gently in his chair and appeared lost in the haze. Then she returned her frightened eyes to Weston and said, "You won't make me go back there? You promise?"

"You don't have to go anywhere you're in danger, Dani. I promise."

She nodded one last time. "Okay."

"Who or what were you running from?"

"The Mission," she said. "I was running away from The Mission."

7

The Mission.

Kate thought back to the news report they had seen three nights ago about the murder that had pointed them in the direction of Brunswick in the first place. The comment at the end of the report about the millions of acres of virgin forest surrounding the city, and how any number of cults could be operating in anonymity.

Could that be it? Could something have happened to this poor girl at a cult community located in the middle of nowhere that would explain her extreme fear?

That scenario would certainly explain the condition of her clothes and her extreme hunger. Walking out of a camp in these woods with no more than the vaguest sense of where to go would be a daunting challenge for an adult, never mind a young girl.

Even the name, "The Mission," conjured in Kate's mind a vaguely religious feel, evoking a tone that felt half spiritual and half sinister. But even if true, it would not explain the tattoo on Dani's inner wrist. The same tattoo worn by the Beast.

Or would it?

One step at a time.

Right now they needed to calm their new friend. The flash of good humor she had shown a moment ago was gone, and there was no reason to frighten her any more than she already was.

Extracting information was one thing; it was a necessary step toward running down the Beast. But terrifying a young girl beyond all reason was another matter entirely, and Kate felt a hot rush of shame. Whatever Dani had been through, she didn't deserve to relive it inside a rundown restaurant in the middle of a small city in central Maine in the company of people she had only just met.

Kate glanced at Weston, ready to interrupt him and tell him enough was enough, that they would have to be satisfied—for now —with what they had already learned.

But it wouldn't be necessary. His expression made very clear he was thinking the same thing, and he nodded slightly, acknowledging her unspoken concern.

He said, "Thank you, Dani. I know this was hard for you, and I'm sorry. But look at Kate. See her across the table?"

The young girl shot a glance in Kate's direction and then lowered her gaze before Kate could even offer a reassuring smile. Then she nodded.

"Kate used to be a police officer. She knows how to protect children—and adults, for that matter—from people who want to harm them. And I've gotten pretty good at helping her. Between the two of us, we'll make sure nobody from The Mission or anywhere else hurts you. Does that sound fair?"

The girl nodded again and sighed deeply. Then she picked up her fork and resumed eating her pie and ice cream. Kate glanced at Christopher and was surprised to see he had stopped rocking and was sitting perfectly still, his face raised toward the ceiling.

Kate breathed deeply and looked around the interior of the Lobster Claw. No one seemed to be paying them any attention.

But her intuition that it was time to stop pushing Dani had been spot on, because the waitress was even now crossing the dining room with a slip of paper in her hand that had to be the check. If she had done so just two minutes earlier, Kate thought they might have had some explaining to do.

And becoming the center of attention was not the way they wanted to start their time in Brunswick.

The waitress, a slightly overweight middle-aged woman with a perpetual smile carved into her blocky face, stopped at the table and said, "Anything else I can get you folks today?"

She did an almost imperceptible double take when glancing at Dani, probably because of the girl's expression. She didn't say anything, but her smile disappeared, only to return a second later like the sun popping out from behind a small cloud.

"No, we're good," Weston said as he reached for the check.

The waitress handed it over and said, "Alrighty then, have a nice day," and as she pivoted and began crossing the dining room toward the kitchen, Kate had a sudden thought.

"Excuse me, miss." Kate pushed her chair back and stood.

The waitress took a couple of steps back toward the table, which was exactly the opposite of what Kate wanted. Kate moved to her and gestured her toward the kitchen until they were out of earshot of the table. Dani didn't need to hear her question. She was already upset enough.

The waitress's surprise was obvious, and she faced Kate with raised eyebrows.

"Are you familiar with Brunswick?" Kate asked.

"I certainly hope so. I've lived here my entire life, which amounts to a lot more years than I'm normally comfortable admitting."

Kate smiled. "Then maybe you can help me. Have you ever heard of something called 'The Mission'? It might be an organization of some kind, or a place, or it might be something completely —"

"Everybody from around here knows what The Mission is. I suspected that's why you're here."

Kate frowned now. "What do you mean?"

The waitress gestured toward Christopher. "Your son. I assume he's the reason you're asking."

"Why would you think that?"

"The Mission is what the locals call the MHCSN, because the actual name of the place is so darn long."

"Okay," Kate said slowly. "And what is the MHCSN?"

The waitress seemed bewildered by the question. "It's the Maine Home for Children with Special Needs."

Kate felt her mouth drop open. She began to speak and stopped. Special needs.

"O-Oh... of course," she stuttered. "How stupid of me. I've never been good with acronyms and the whole 'Mission' thing threw me off. Makes perfect sense now, thank you."

The waitress stared at her a moment, an odd look on her face, then smiled and said, "My pleasure," and walked away.

8

Outside the Lobster Claw, Dani again took Christopher's hand and led him to the car. It was done naturally, seemingly without conscious thought, as though caring for another was second nature to the girl.

As they ushered the children into the Rambler, Weston said, "What was all that with the waitress?"

Kate shot a glance toward Dani, then told the kids to hang on. She gestured to Weston and they walked a few paces away for privacy. She kept her voice low. "I took a shot that she might have heard of The Mission. The way Dani was acting, I thought it might be a religious cult or something."

"I had the same thought."

"Well, we were both wrong. It's an acronym. MHCSN. It stands for the Maine Home for Children with Special Needs."

Weston's eyes registered surprise. "Where LeBlanc was killed."

Kate nodded. "That would explain Dani's fear of the place. She's a murder witness."

Weston's brow creased. "That's a bit of a leap."

"Seriously? She told us she didn't want to 'go back' to The Mission. Which means she had to have been there in the first place. Her obvious terror at the prospect of returning means she saw something that frightened her very badly. Add that to LeBlanc getting his tongue cut out and that tattoo on her wrist and I don't think it's much of a leap at all. She was there that night."

Kate felt they needed to push the girl harder. Find out her home address, notify her parents that she was safe, then accompany her to the Brunswick Police Department. The sooner the better.

"There's just one problem with your theory," Weston said. "That girl is not in any way, shape or form, a special needs kid."

"Haven't you noticed how she interacts with Chris? He scares the crap out of most kids her age, or at least makes them uneasy because he's so different. He didn't faze her in the least. She took to him like a duck to water."

Kate saw the flicker in Weston's eyes as the realization hit him.

"She knows somebody at the home," he said. "A family member. Maybe somebody on staff. Or even one of the kids."

Kate nodded. "And if my instincts are right, the police will need to speak with her. They have the resources to find out what she knows and to keep her protected. Resources we simply can't—"

"Can we slow down a bit?" Weston said, raising his voice.

They both glanced toward the car and saw that Dani was staring out her window at the passing traffic, oblivious to their conversation.

Weston lowered his tone. "You're looking at this from the perspective of a cop. Step outside that persona for a minute. Once we release that girl to the authorities, we'll never see her again. We'll lose all access to information that we need just as much—if not more—than the police."

Kate started to speak but Weston held his hand up.

"Let me finish. Yes, we'll take her to the authorities. Of course we will. But it's been almost three full days since the night of the murder. If she's been missing all that time, adding a few more hours won't hurt the police as much as it'll help us."

Kate realized that this had been her exact line of thinking before she shifted into concerned cop mode. She sighed and didn't answer.

"Besides," Weston said. "I don't get the feeling anyone's even looking for her."

"Why would you say that?"

"A young girl's disappearance is a big deal. TV stations break into their regular programming with AMBER alerts, the missing child's face gets plastered all over television. Bulletins are issued on the radio and on freeway signs. Brunswick isn't a large city, Kate. Even in the short time we've been here, don't you think we would have seen or heard *something* if the authorities were looking for her? At the very least, somebody in that restaurant would have recognized her and started asking questions."

"You've got a point," she said. "And if the cops *aren't* looking for her, that means they don't know anything about her. It also means her parents haven't bothered to report her missing."

"Exactly. And given all of the above, wouldn't it be to our benefit to hang on to this child a few more hours? Just a few? Nobody knows where she is, which means she'll be perfectly safe with—"

Noah's right. We can't take her home yet.

They looked toward the Rambler again and saw Christopher staring in their direction now, Dani still watching the traffic roll by. Walking away from the car had gained them privacy from the girl, but of course Chris had been privy to their entire conversation.

Why not? Kate asked him. *Her parents must be worried sick about her.*

She had been about to agree with Weston, but with Chris present and engaged, his input could be critical. She wanted his take.

I don't know. Everything's jumbled and impossible to read. But Dani has a big part to play in whatever's happening here. And I still think the Beast is near. I can feel him. We need to keep Dani close.

"You heard the man," Weston said. "So I assume it's unanimous?"

Kate nodded, and as they headed for the car, she continued to keep her voice low. "Why would the Beast still be here? What kind of twisted game is he playing?"

Weston shook his head. "I don't know. But I have a feeling we're going to find out."

The motel was like any of a hundred other places they had stayed in all across the country. Old. Cheaply constructed. Bare-bones. If not for the framed print of a schooner at full sail hanging crooked-ly on one wall, they could just as easily have been in Houston or Boise or Cleveland.

They took a pair of adjoining rooms, each with two single beds. The plan was for Weston to sleep in one room with Christopher, and Kate would share a room with Dani. But the two children had snuggled up together on one of the beds in Kate's room a little while ago, Dani wrapping her arms around Chris in an embrace that would have convinced any onlooker that the young girl was the disabled boy's sister.

A protective sister.

Within minutes, both had fallen fast asleep, and instantly the plan changed. Unless one awoke and wanted to move to his or her own bed, they would stay where they were until morning. Kate didn't think she had ever seen Christopher so calm, so serene, and Dani seemed to draw strength from the blind boy who had not spoken a single word to her since they met.

Kate watched them for a moment, then turned to Weston, again keeping her voice low. "The girl's certainly taken to Christopher, but she doesn't completely trust us yet. It could be a while before we get any answers from her."

"So we do whatever it takes," Weston said. "The odds of that tattoo on her wrist being unrelated to the Beast are roughly equivalent to the odds of hitting the lottery and getting struck by lightning on the same day. Hell, at the same time."

Kate nodded. "Maybe while we're waiting for her to warm up to us, I can drop by the Brunswick PD, see what kind of information I can gather about the murder."

Weston shook his head. "Bad idea. Once you approach them, we're immediately and forever on their radar."

"I'm a licensed PI now, remember? Cops are used to getting requests for information from private investigators."

"And what case are you going to tell them you're working? Think about it for a second. PI or not, any mention of LeBlanc is likely to arouse their suspicion. We don't know the area, don't know the people, don't know the facts of the case anywhere near well enough for you to go in there and sound believable."

Kate felt her temper rising. "I can come up with something, trust me."

"Until we know what's happening here, I think we should

concentrate on staying as far away from the police and the official murder investigation as possible."

"Well then, what's your suggestion?"

Before Weston could respond, a voice filled Kate's head.

Use me.

She stiffened in surprise and saw Weston doing the same thing. They had been certain both children were asleep, and even now, the kids were unmoving, still lying in the same positions they'd been in since crawling on top of the bedcovers.

Weston raised his voice slightly, although doing so wasn't necessary. Christopher had obviously heard them just fine before. "Did we wake you?"

I wasn't sleeping. This isn't comfortable.

Weston glanced at Kate in surprise. "You can move into your own bed any time you want, Chris. I thought you knew that."

I'm staying here because she needs this.

It was a simple statement, offered innocently, and Kate felt her eyes begin to well up. She turned quickly away from Weston. She didn't want him seeing her weakness. But that small act of selfless kindness shown by a boy who had seen so much death and such horror in his short life touched her in a way she would never have guessed she could be touched.

Weston held his gaze on her for just a moment and she knew that he knew. But to his credit he made no mention of it. Instead he said to Christopher, "I think we're on the same page about using you. I was just about to suggest it to Kate."

"Suggest what?" she asked.

You both know I lived in a place just like The Mission, Chris said. *I can be your way in. You two can be my mom and dad taking me there for a visit because you're considering having me live there.*

Kate shook her head. "You think I haven't thought of that? A man was killed, Chris, and there's every indication that the Beast killed him. No way am I gonna let you get near that place. We've already put you in the line of fire too many times."

You haven't done anything I didn't want you to do.

"Maybe so, but I still don't like it."

What choice do we have? Dani isn't ready to talk yet, and the longer we wait, the more chance the Beast has of getting away again.

"Assuming he's still here," Weston said.

He's here. I told you that.

"Look," Kate said, "Nobody wants to catch this guy more than I do, but—"

Stop trying to protect me, Kate. How many times do I have to prove to you that I can take care of myself?

She lifted her eyebrows and looked at Weston. Despite her instinct to resist, Chris's idea did make perfect sense, and the fact that he had been the first one to suggest it made it a little easier to accept.

She sighed. "I guess you're right."

Good. We can go first thing in the morning.

Kate shook her head. "Not until we get Dani squared away. If we can pry her address out of her, we'll take her home, then go back and try to question her later. Otherwise—"

No. Dani has to come with us.

"Chris, I know you like her. I can tell she likes you, too. But that won't work. She's terrified of The Mission. Remember how upset she got when she thought we were going to take her back there?"

I know, but sooner or later she'll open up and we need to know what she saw. If we take her home, we may never get this close to her again.

"Fair enough," Kate said. "But taking her to the scene of her trauma seems like a bad idea. She made it pretty clear how she feels."

She needs to be with us.

Kate looked at Weston questioningly.

Why was Chris so insistent about keeping Dani close?

His conviction that the girl was at the center of whatever was happening here would explain it to a point, but she believed there might be more to it than that.

Weston met her gaze.

"Later," he mouthed silently.

"So, let's hear it," Kate said to Weston. "You obviously have a theory about what's happening between those two."

Christopher had finally fallen asleep, and while Kate understood Weston's desire not to discuss the subject in front of the boy, she knew opportunities to talk without being overheard were relatively rare.

"Lucy," he said simply.

"What's that supposed to mean?"

"Chris has mentioned any number of times how he believes the Beast is still close by, but what hasn't he made any mention of at all?"

"Lucy," Kate said, nodding. "But he also said he can't get a handle on what he's receiving, that everything is jumbled and unintelligible. Maybe that's why he isn't feeling her."

"Maybe," Weston conceded. "But I don't think so. Their bond was pretty strong. Even in his confusion I think he'd be able to sense her."

"Okay, but what does all of this have to do with his latching onto Dani? If he was a few years older, I'd say he was infatuated with her."

"I think you're more right than you realize. He's not infatuated in the sense of falling in love, at least not as adults understand it. But I believe he's transferring his feelings for Lucy onto Dani. He misses Lucy, he's not in contact with her, and he's worried about her. All of those feelings are coming out in how he relates to Dani."

Kate considered Weston's words. They made sense. She had been so wrapped up in the mystery of Dani Melanson, and the tattoo, and what the girl's relationship to the Beast might be, that she hadn't given Lucy any thought at all.

Lucy had been Chris's best friend at the group home they'd lived in. The Beast had taken her with him after the brutal attack that had claimed Christopher's tongue, and Chris's desire to find her was as strong as his desire to punish the Beast. She and Chris had been in contact telepathically until the signal had been abruptly severed months ago in Alabama.

And he missed her.

Was worried about her.

And Kate, in her single-minded need to run down the man who had killed her mother, to put an end once and for all to his sick, lethal games, had forgotten that other things mattered, too.

Christopher's feelings were foremost among them.

Kate vowed to keep that in mind moving forward.

9

Kate had hoped that after a good night's sleep, Dani Melanson would be more forthcoming.

It wasn't to be, however. She seemed cheerful, and much more comfortable in their company than she was yesterday, but remained tight-lipped when it came to sharing anything about herself.

This was becoming a concern, because Kate had done a little Internet research while everyone else was asleep and discovered dozens upon dozens of "Melansons" living in the Brunswick area. If the girl didn't choose to reveal her address, there would be virtually no way for them to guess it.

It was also possible she had lied.

Maybe Melanson wasn't even her last name.

Weston had gotten up early and gone out to pick up coffee, juice, and donuts. By the time he returned, everyone was up and showered, even Dani. Her hair shone and she was scrubbed clean, dressed in a pair of Kate's shorts and a t-shirt scrounged out of her suitcase.

The clothes were only slightly too big for her, and considerably more modest than what she'd been wearing when they'd first encountered her. They served to emphasize her tender age, and Kate shook her head thinking about how lucky the girl had been not to be picked up by the wrong driver.

The group sat around a rickety writing table enjoying their breakfast, and Weston nodded to Dani. "How did you sleep last night?"

Christopher had, true to his word, stayed next to her until morning.

"Good," she said. "Better than I have in a long time."

"I'm glad to hear it. But now it's time to talk about getting you home. Your mom and dad must be worried sick about you."

She's staying with us, Christopher said.

His resolve obviously hadn't weakened overnight.

Calm down, Kate told him. *We promised to figure something out and we will.*

Dani's response to Weston wasn't much of a surprise. "Can't I stay with you a little longer?"

"Dani..."

"Just until this afternoon?"

"We're not from around here," Weston said. "And we came to Maine because there are some things we have to do."

"Things like what?"

"Nothing you need to worry about. But our first stop is The Mission."

Dani's expression abruptly shifted, sudden stress evident in the high pitch of her voice. "Why? Because of Christopher?"

Weston hesitated. "It's complicated. But you made it pretty clear yesterday that you had no interest in going there. In fact, you seemed pretty afraid of the place."

"I... I don't want to talk about that."

"Any particular reason?"

"I-I just don't. I wish I'd never heard of that place. And I wish my bro..." She slammed her mouth closed and looked down at the surface of the table, looking as if she had been caught with her hand in the cookie jar.

Kate shared a glance with Weston.

His voice was gentle when he spoke. "You were about to say your brother, weren't you, Dani? Your brother is a patient at The Mission."

For a long moment Dani sat frozen in her chair, her eyes focused resolutely downward. Then she nodded without speaking.

"Were you there the night Peter LaBlanc was killed? Is that why you're scared? You were visiting your brother that night?"

A second nod.

"And you're afraid of going back there, but you're concerned about him?"

"Yes." Her voice wavered with the single syllable. It sounded small and fearful to Kate, and emphasized the fact that she was nearly as young as Chris.

Weston cleared his throat. Kate sensed he might start asking questions about the tattoo and wanted to warn him to take it slow, but he simply shook his head and gestured to her and Chris. "Well, like I said, the three of us need to go there. And if you like, we can check on your brother and make sure he's okay. Does that sound reasonable to you?"

Dani raised her eyes from the table. They were red-rimmed and watery. "Thank you," she said quietly.

"You're welcome. But that leaves us with a bit of an issue. Since the three of us are going and you won't be joining us, we'll have to —"

She stays with us.

"I know that," Weston said reflexively, surprise making him blurt the words out without thinking.

A look of confusion crossed Dani's face. "You know what?"

"Never mind," Kate said. "It's not important. But I have an idea. How about you stay here at the motel and keep an eye on our stuff while we're gone? Would you be willing to do that?"

Dani's eyes widened and she nodded, this time out of excitement. "I would love that. " She held up a worn and dog-eared copy of THE HUNGER GAMES. "I found this in our nightstand drawer. I'll bet I can get halfway through it while you're gone!"

Kate couldn't help but smile at her enthusiasm. It was infectious. The girl seemed incapable of hiding her feelings, and when she got excited or happy she had a personality that sparkled.

Weston caught Kate's eye and said, "Can we talk?"

Dani dropped her nose into the book as Weston stood and crossed into the adjoining room, gesturing for Kate to follow.

Once they were out of earshot, he said, "Are you sure it's a good idea to have her stay here by herself?"

"Why not? She's obviously pretty self-sufficient. I think she can handle an hour or two inside a locked, safe motel room."

"I'm not worried about her being able to stay by herself. I'm more concerned that we'll get back and she'll be gone. And if that happens, *then* where are we? We'll never get any answers from her."

"Relax," Kate said. "She's got a good thing going right now and she knows it. She's not going anywhere."

Kate's right, Christopher told them. He was still sitting at the breakfast table, but as usual, that made no difference. *She'll be here when we get back.*

"If you're worried about it," Kate said to Weston, "maybe you should talk to her a little more before we go. She's starting to open up a little. Maybe we can find out what happened to her that night."

"Or shut her down completely. You saw how scared she was. I don't think she's all that anxious to tell us much more."

"Let's find out."

They crossed into the adjoining room, strolled back to the little table, and Weston sat down next to Dani. All the skepticism he had shown just a moment ago seemed to have disappeared.

"Okay," he said to Dani. "You can stay here while we visit The Mission, but in return, you need to give us a little information. That seems only fair, don't you think?"

The girl didn't answer. She simply gazed back at him expectantly.

"Let's start with the easy stuff first. I need to know where you live so we can take you home when it's time."

Dani stiffened immediately and Weston raised his hands in a calming gesture. "I don't mean now. We already agreed that you could stay here for awhile. But eventually you're going to have to go home, and this seems as good a time as any for us to find out your address."

She sighed deeply and shifted her gaze from Weston to Kate and back to Weston. "Fine," she said with the look of someone convinced she was making a grievous error in judgment. "Depot Road in Lisbon."

"House number?"

The frown vanished from her face, replaced by a look of amusement. "There aren't any house numbers, silly. You just drive on Depot Road until you come to our trailer."

"Oh, okay." Weston grinned at her. "My bad. And your parents' names?"

"Maureen and Tom."

"Would you like to call them and let them know you're okay? They must be very worried."

She shook her head. "We don't have a phone. And why would they be worried? It's only been a few days. I wasn't due home for a week."

Weston glanced up at Kate, his confusion evident. "A week? Where do they think you are?"

"At The Mission."

"You were supposed to spend a whole week there?"

"Sure. I do it all the time."

"But what about the murder? It's been all over the news and I'd think that would scare your folks half to death. About you *and* your brother."

She shook her head again. "Our TV is broken. And even if it wasn't, they'd never watch the news." She lifted her shoulders in a resigned shrug. "They don't care about much of anything."

Kate and Weston exchanged a look. Was Dani lying, or could her parents really be that apathetic about their own children?

But Kate knew the answer. She'd seen worse in her time as a cop.

"Okay," Weston said. "Now that we've got that cleared up, tell me a little bit about that tattoo on your wrist. Did you get that at The Mission on the night Mr. LeBlanc was killed?"

Her eyes grew wide and her teeth ground together. She nodded unhappily.

"Who gave it to you? Was it a man? A stranger?"

She nodded again, tears gathering in her eyes.

"Can you describe him to me?"

The tears spilled down her cheeks. "He was big and ugly and mean."

"What about his hair? His eyes? What color were they?"

She thought about this. "...I...I don't remember."

"He leaned over you giving you a tattoo, but you can't remember his hair color?"

No answer.

"How about his clothing," Weston said, trying a different tack, and Kate sensed his growing frustration. "How was the man dressed?"

Dani shook her head. "I don't remember."

You have to stop now. She's not ready for this.

Weston shot a glance toward Christopher, then pushed his seat back and stepped away from the table. He walked to the door and stepped outside, breathing deeply of the fresh air as he tried to control his temper.

Kate moved to the spot he had just vacated and spoke in what she hoped was a soothing tone. "You can't remember or you don't want to talk about it?"

Dani shook her head. "I just can't remember. I would tell you if I could, I swear."

"Did he make you look away while he was working on your tattoo?"

Another shake of the head.

Weston had heard Dani talking and stepped back inside. He closed the door and leaned against it, watching the exchange with interest.

The Beast did something to her, Chris said. *He's making her forget.*

Kate realized she had been wondering the same thing. The Beast's face had been inches from Dani's for however long it took to ink her wrist. No matter how fearful she had been at the time, it was absurd to think she would not have noticed *something* about her tormentor's physical appearance.

So was the Beast now using some form of mind control? Like that freak of an old man they'd encountered in Michigan who got his jollies playing make-believe inside people's heads?

Could he really have a way of blocking people's perception of him? Of making them forget?

It was impossible to believe.

Kate believed it.

10

The man with the tattoo was getting sick and tired of sitting around doing nothing.

He had known he might have to wait awhile for his pursuers to arrive, and in reality, the down time hadn't even been that long yet. Not even four full days.

But sitting in a car with his thumb up his ass wasn't something he was used to doing. He didn't like waiting. Waiting made his scalp itch. It made his skin crawl. It made him feel...twitchy.

And he didn't like feeling twitchy. He was a man of action. A man who preferred seeing others dance to his tune over waiting for the fiddler to show.

He hated waiting. For anything.

Still, this particular wait had the potential to be well worth the itchy scalp and the crawly skin. It had been a long time since he had been challenged in any way. A very long time. Because in general, people were stupid. They were ill-informed and ignorant, slow to recognize danger and even slower to defend themselves against it.

When he really thought about it—and what else could he do but think while sitting here doing nothing?—it was a miracle human beings were even still around.

Natural selection, my ass, he thought. As far as he was concerned, Darwin had been full of shit because had he been right, the human race would have disappeared centuries ago.

The man with the tattoo shifted in his seat, never letting his gaze wander from the front entrance of The Mission. When his pursuers arrived here—as he knew they would eventually—this would be where they'd make their appearance.

They were as predictable as they were foolish.

And foolish for thinking they would ever catch him.

There *was* no risk of being caught. The man with the tattoo was so highly evolved, mentally as well as physically, that his pursuers' amateurish attempts to seek him out and exact retribution for their perceived grievances was pointless.

It was laughable.

Pathetic.

Doomed to failure.

They were like a ten-year-old chess novice attempting to take on a grand master. He could toy with them as long as he wanted and finish them off any time he chose.

He sighed deeply and sipped from a bottle of vitamin water. Good God, this was boring. He thought about changing locations— he had discovered long ago that the key to remaining invisible while managing successful surveillance was to change locations often, to never stay in one place long enough to arouse the suspicions of onlookers—and then decided to wait a little longer before doing so.

This area was a little tricky in the sense that there weren't many spots he could utilize and still maintain the line of sight he needed. But if potential surveillance locations were limited, so too were potential witnesses. The Mission was located in an industrial area of Brunswick, filled with crumbling factories and aging warehouses, many of them empty and abandoned, rust-pocked shells that had long since been forgotten, relegated to the dustbin of history.

In other words, this was not exactly a bustling center of commerce.

At the moment, he was parked behind an ancient Quonset hut with broken-out windows and a partially collapsed roof. He had nosed the front of his vehicle out from behind the building just far enough to allow a full, unobstructed view of The Mission's front gate.

At a distance of several hundred yards, he wouldn't be able to see the interior of their vehicle with the naked eye when they finally showed up, but that wouldn't matter. Their car was instantly recognizable, a half-century-old white station wagon that would stick out like a sore thumb the minute they stopped at the gate. And the distance meant there was virtually no chance they would catch sight of him.

He sipped again at his water and glanced at his surroundings. The area still appeared deserted. He took his eyes off the front gate for no more than five seconds, but when he returned his attention to it, a broad smile creased his face.

The old station wagon was here. Finally.

He lifted a pair of Nikon Monarch 7 binoculars off the front seat and raised the eyepieces to his face. The binocs were expensive, relatively speaking, more product than he probably needed for his purposes, but part of what made him invincible was exhaustive preparation, and given the fact that surveillance was such an important part of his day-to-day existence, he felt the expense had been more than justified.

The wagon rolled to a stop at the gate, and his eyes narrowed as he examined the interior with the glasses. What he saw inside the car was exactly what he had been expecting to see: two deluded adults and a child who should have been long dead.

But something had changed, and an odd sensation prickled his scalp. He lowered the glasses for a moment, then raised them again, taking another look inside the wagon.

Only three people. Man, woman and child.

Yet... He could *feel* the presence of another.

Someone who didn't belong.

A wild card.

He let the sensation wash over him like a waterfall. He wasn't even sure himself how his psychic abilities worked. He certainly couldn't have described the process to an onlooker. But he trusted the feelings implicitly. Feelings he had been relying on for longer than he could remember, way back into the misty recesses of history.

His eyes glazed and his mind narrowed to a razor-sharp focus as the feelings came. And then he knew who the wild card was, who had either joined or been in contact with these three—and recently at that.

The girl.

The one who had been inside The Mission on the night of his sortie. He had been instantly suspicious of her, because it was obvious to him she didn't belong there. That she was not like the others. There was nothing "special needs" about her.

But he had continued to execute his plan despite this unexpected appearance. Even the most thoroughly planned ops encountered unanticipated occurrences. It was inevitable. And despite his curiosity regarding the girl's presence that night, she clearly had not represented a threat to him.

This scenario, however, was something different entirely.

How had she ended up in the company of these three, and what did this mean to him?

How much of what she observed that night had she told them? And if she had joined them...

Where was she now?

His eyes remained glued to the ancient station wagon as he considered the potential ramifications of this development. And while the mystery of how that young girl had wound up allied with these three pathetic wannabes was interesting in a theoretical way, he concluded it changed nothing.

In fact, rather than being a negative, it might represent an unexpected opportunity, a chance for him to drive home a point he had gone to so much trouble to make.

A plan insinuated itself into his brain, fully formed and brilliant, and for the second time in little more than a minute, the man with the tattoo felt a smile slide across his face.

Unexpected opportunities were the best kind.

11

The wrought iron gate outside The Mission was closed, a small call box mounted at car door height on a sturdy brick post to one side of it. A cast iron plaque fastened to the fence read MAINE HOME FOR CHILDREN WITH SPECIAL NEEDS in gold script.

The crime scene tape that had been so prominent in the television news report was gone, leaving no sign that a murder had recently occurred here. Anyone who wasn't aware of that fact would never have known.

Weston eased up to the call box and rolled down his window. He unlatched the cover, lifted the telephone handset from its cradle, and held it to his ear.

After a moment he said, "Yes, hello. My name is Noah Karlson. My wife Kate and I are looking for a place for our son and we were hoping you might be able to spare a few minutes to answer a few questions and perhaps show us around your facility."

Weston listened a moment, then said, "Sorry, but we've been on the road and weren't exactly sure when we would arrive, so we didn't want to waste your time by making an appointment we might not be able to keep."

He listened again and said, "Of course. His name is Christopher and he's eleven."

He turned to Kate and winked as he said into the phone, "That would be wonderful. Thanks so much for your hospitality."

Weston replaced the handset on its cradle and swung the call box door closed. A second later the gate began to swing slowly open. When there was sufficient clearance, Weston accelerated onto the property and the Rambler crept along the short, pothole-strewn driveway. After fifty or so feet it widened out into the small parking lot they had seen on the news report footage.

Being the middle of the day, cars took up the majority of the spots, but they managed to find an empty one marked VISITOR.

They pulled in and Kate turned to face Chris.

"Are you sure you're okay to be here? This setting, this situation, it's all so similar to the one from your past. Would you rather stay in the car?"

I'll be okay, he said after a lengthy pause. It lasted so long Kate had begun to fear he was gone into the haze.

She sensed uneasiness lurking behind his statement. Uncertainty. It was a significant change for a young boy who was typically unflappable and calm, almost Zen-like.

"If you change your mind, if you start to feel uncomfortable in any way, let us know and we'll get you out of there."

I know Kate, and thank you. But it's important I be a part of this.

Weston pocketed the Rambler's key and faced the back seat as well. "Why do I get the feeling you're holding out on us, Chris? Something's bothering you. What is it?"

The boy was quiet again for a long moment.

It... it's him. The Beast. He's near. I can feel him.

"Here?" Kate blurted. "He's at The Mission?"

I don't know. Everything's still blurry and indistinct. But I can feel him.

The car fell silent as they considered the significance of Christopher's words. Could this be a stroke of incredible good fortune? Were they getting close to stopping the Beast once and for all?

Or was it a trap?

What the hell were they about to walk into?

"Let's get moving," Weston said. "We have work to do, and sitting inside the car isn't getting us any closer to finishing it."

Kate climbed out of the car, took Christopher by the hand and turned toward the entrance. Weston fell in next to her and as they approached the building she said, "Noah and Kate Karlson?"

He shrugged. "I improvised."

"Why didn't you just use your real last name?"

Another shrug. "Defense mechanism? That tattoo on Dani's

wrist has me spooked, I guess. And now, with Chris sensing the Beast, I'm thinking if anything goes sour here, the less evidence we leave behind, the better."

"Believe me," Kate said, "I'm all for anonymity. But did it occur to you that the staff might ask for ID?"

He stopped and faced her. "Not until just now."

"They've lost an employee to murder, Noah, so they may be a tad sensitive about who they let inside. Improvising is fine, but it helps to think things through a bit, too."

He frowned. "I hate it when you're right."

"I know you do, but let's hope *this* time I'm wrong."

She plastered a smile on her face and they continued walking.

As they approached the door, a middle-aged woman swung it open and said, "Good afternoon, folks, my name is Jane Hamilton. I'm the administrator here at The Mission, and I'll be your guide today." She looked at Chris. "This must be Christopher."

She ruffled his hair, then offered them perfunctory handshakes before turning and leading them inside the facility.

No mention of any IDs, thank god.

The woman was large but not fat, and Kate guessed she would think of herself as big-boned. She appeared to be in her late fifties, with steel-gray hair, a conservative suit, and a no-nonsense demeanor. Frosty, almost.

She also seemed preoccupied, and it struck Kate that she certainly had the right to be.

They entered the building and were transported straight into the 1950s. Dingy light green linoleum tiles on the floor and matching—more or less—paint on the cinderblock walls reminded Kate of a prison or an insane asylum, rather than a modern care facility. She was about to ask the building's age when Hamilton spoke first.

"So," she said, glancing back as she walked. "What makes you feel you might need to avail yourselves of our facility? Most of the children we get are either orphaned or so severely challenged their parents are not able to provide their care. It looks as though that's not really an issue with Christopher."

"Unfortunately," Weston said, "It's a matter of economics. We can no longer afford for Kate to stay home and care for Chris. We need a second income to make ends meet, and given the cost of home care, we feel it might be best to at least consider other options."

"Home care for these children *is* expensive," she agreed, shooting him an odd look—almost one of suspicion. "But I must admit I'm a bit surprised to see you here."

"Why is that?"

"I assume you've watched the news and know what happened outside our gates the other night?"

Weston and Kate exchanged a quick glance and Kate said, "Yes, of course. An unfortunate tragedy."

"Quite so," Hamilton said. "And even though it was clearly a random act, I assumed it would be some time before any parents showed up on our doorstep looking to house a child. Most would be scared away by such an incident."

Weston nodded. "Unfortunately, it's a violent world. But like I said, we're simply weighing options. And to be frank, The Mission is one of the more affordable options we've considered."

The look of suspicion returned but was gone in a second as they reached the end of a long hallway.

She paused in front of a glass-walled office that looked as if it belonged to a high school principal, or maybe a precinct captain in a big city police station. A receptionist's desk stood empty outside and Hamilton noticed Kate looking at it.

"My assistant only works part of the day," she said. "With recent budget cuts, we simply can't afford to maintain someone full-time." She took a deep breath and continued. "Would you like to take the tour before we talk? I'm afraid it'll have to be an abbreviated one. We're very busy at the moment."

"That's fine," Kate said, wondering where all the children were. Wondering where the Beast was. Except for Hamilton, they hadn't seen a single person since entering the building.

That all changed after they descended a stairwell at the end of the hallway. At the bottom of the stairs, they passed through double swinging doors into a large, brightly lit room. About a dozen children ranging in age from very young—perhaps four or five—to late teens were spread throughout the room. They were currently working on arts and crafts projects at several tables, three or four children to a table, with a pair of counselors moving between the kids, offering encouragement, and stopping to help those who needed it.

"This is our cafeteria," Hamilton said. "Between meals it also serves as a multipurpose room, where we work on projects and play a number of games. It's very handy during the cold Maine winters, when venturing outside is not a realistic option."

Kate was again reminded of Michigan and the cold winter that had almost claimed their lives, but pushed the thought from her mind. She only half-listened to the rest of Hamilton's running commentary, more concerned with another matter.

Chris? Are you okay?

Silence.

Chris? Did you hear me?

Yes, he said. *I'm fine.*

Are you still sensing the Beast?

Oh, yes.

Any idea where he might be or what he might be doing?

No. But I don't think he's inside the building with us.

Kate couldn't decide whether this was good news or bad.

They strolled through the room, approaching one of the tables where the kids were hard at work cutting colored construction paper into shapes—some recognizable, others not—and then gluing those shapes onto heavier-grade construction paper. A few of them glanced up curiously as they passed, but most paid them no attention.

Kate watched as a young boy roughly Christopher's age placed what may or may not have been a dog onto his construction paper and pressed it down, holding it in place for a few seconds. He was the picture of concentration, his tongue hanging out of his mouth as he worked. His skinny arms stuck out of a long-sleeved Boston Bruins t-shirt, which struck her as a little odd. The heater was pumping pretty good down here—so why the long sleeves?

As the boy lifted his hand off the paper, Kate got her answer and gasped.

Despite her history as a police officer, despite the things she had seen and experienced since teaming up with Weston and Chris, despite her natural tendency to stay in control, she gasped.

Simply could not stop it from escaping.

Because peeking out from under one of the boy's sleeves was a crude tattoo of a circle with a dot in the middle.

12

Kate stared in shock at the boy's arm as time seemed to slow.

He swiped the back of his hand across his forehead to clear away a trickle of sweat and she followed the motion with her eyes, zoned in on that goddamned tattoo.

What the hell?

She stopped walking, freezing in place as if she had grown roots. Chris took one step forward, still holding her hand, and then he stopped as well. He could sense her surprise.

What is it, Kate? Are you okay?

She barely heard him, her thoughts whirling, her mind a million miles away. She dragged her gaze from the boy, glanced at Weston and knew that he had seen what she had.

She dropped Christopher's hand and moved toward the tattooed boy's table. Toward the three other children, busy with their arts and crafts project. She felt herself walking sluggishly, as if underwater.

What's wrong, Kate?

Christopher sounded insistent but she ignored him. For the first time, she noticed that *all* of the children were dressed in long sleeves, and an icy dread gripped her heart.

She stopped at the table, extended her arm and grasped the sleeve of the boy closest to her. He was older than the first one, and seemed more developmentally challenged, and at Kate's touch, he simply stopped what he was doing and gaped at her dully.

She gently eased his sleeve up toward his elbow, not wanting to see what would be revealed but doing it anyway. Her mouth went dry and she felt her eyes widen, as little by little, a circle was revealed, inked into the white skin of the boy's inner wrist.

A circle with a dot in the middle.

Numb, Kate reached for another child's arm. This boy tried to pull away but she was able to lift the sleeve enough to confirm what she already knew was there.

Then the last boy at the table. Same thing.

And Kate knew. Every last child inside this facility had been tattooed with the very same image.

The circumpunct.

A young staff member, who was helping a child at the next table, looked up at Kate with a half-smile that vanished the moment she saw Kate holding the boy's sleeve.

"Hey!" she said sharply. "You can't touch the children. Take your hands off him."

She couldn't have been more than twenty or so, with short-cropped black hair and a tiny diamond stud protruding from her left nostril—a fashion statement that had likely caused some friction with her overly officious boss.

Kate locked eyes with her and slowly lifted the boy's arm until the tattoo was visible to her.

"Explain this," she said.

The young woman paled and turned reflexively toward Hamilton, who had continued walking and was several feet ahead, approaching a door at the far end of the room. Hamilton didn't seem inclined to stop moving, didn't even seem inclined to slow down despite having turned to observe that her guests were no longer behind her.

Her eyes darkened and she grimaced. She had to know something was happening between Kate and her staff member. The tension was obvious. But if she did, she didn't give any indication.

She waved them forward and said, "I really don't have much extra time, and remember, you came here without an appointment. We must move things along."

Kate locked eyes with Hamilton and pointedly ignored her. She turned her attention back to the young woman, whose name tag read *Livvie.*

"How many children are full-time residents at this facility?"

The woman looked for help from Hamilton, who was waiting by the door.

"Never mind her," Kate said. "Answer the question."

"Are-are you with the police?"

Kate saw no reason to dissuade her of the notion. "Answer the question. You have nothing to worry about if you answer honestly. How many children?"

"Twelve."

"So all of your residents are here right now?"

Livvie counted heads quickly and said, "Yes, why?"

Kate looked at Livvie's wrist. No tattoo. She didn't recall seeing a tattoo on the other counselor's wrist, either.

"Why are these children tattooed? How did they get them?"

Livvie looked as if she was about to cry. "I... I-I think you'll have to get the answers to those questions from Ms. Hamilton."

"All right," Kate said. "I'll do just that."

Grabbing Chris's hand, she left Livvie behind and marched toward Hamilton, Weston falling in beside her.

Hamilton was still standing near the door, her arms crossed. "I really must insist you keep up. I'm doing you a favor here, and I don't appreciate—"

"We can skip the rest of the tour," Kate said curtly. "We have other things we need to discuss. Right now. Let's take it to your office."

"*Excuse* me?"

"I think you heard the lady," Weston said.

"Who do you think you are, talking to me like this? I can already see that The Mission is *not* a good fit for your child. I'll have to insist you leave now."

"And I'll have to insist we go to your office," Kate said.

"Who *are* you people? Do I need to call the police?"

"Go ahead. And after we talk to them, do you know what our next stop will be?"

Hamilton's eyes flashed, anger simmering just behind them. "I'm sure I don't care where you go, as long as you're out of my facility."

"You'll care when we go straight to the press and inform them that every resident of The Mission has been branded with the mark of a deranged serial killer."

It was a bluff, of course. Kate had no intention of sharing anything about the Beast with the press, the police, or anyone else. But Hamilton didn't need to know that.

The woman stiffened and said nothing for a moment as she regained her composure. The spark of anger had abruptly disappeared, and now she seemed hesitant. Frightened, even.

In fact, she suddenly seemed terrified.

"I... I only have a few minutes," she said.

"That's all we'll need," Weston told her.

She stood there a moment longer, then turned on her heels and exited the multipurpose room.

No one spoke as they walked to her office.

13

"You're the ones, aren't you?"

Hamilton sat behind a cluttered metal desk, her face pale, as she inhaled deeply and blew out a long, shaky breath.

Kate, Weston and Christopher were seated across from her.

"We're *what* ones?" Weston asked.

"I thought you might be. That's why I asked you about the news reports when you first showed up. But you seemed normal enough and I wasn't sure if he was telling the truth."

Kate frowned. "What are you talking about?"

"I was told to expect visitors. Which is the only reason I'm answering your questions."

"Told by whom?"

"By the man who murdered Peter."

Kate and Weston exchanged a look, then Kate glanced at Christopher, who rocked quietly on the chair beside her, seemingly lost in the haze.

"Let me understand this," Weston said. "You *spoke* to LeBlanc's killer? You know who he is?"

"No. I've never met him. I wasn't here on the night of the... intrusion."

Kate raised her hands. "Hang on a second. Let's slow down a little and take this one step at a time. If you weren't here the night LeBlanc was killed, how did this guy communicate with you?"

"He gave a message to a staff member who *was* here. The one he left alive."

"And what's his name?"

"It's a woman. Her name is Livvie Barnstead."

Kate blinked. "Livvie? You mean the girl I just spoke to in the multipurpose room?"

"That's right."

"And she was with the murderer?"

"Yes." Hamilton shuddered. "The poor girl."

"Get her in here, right now. She needs to be part of this discussion."

Livvie Barnstead was no less frightened than Hamilton.

Kate couldn't blame her. If she had come face-to-face with the Beast and was still breathing, she had beaten the odds by a significant margin.

Barnstead refused the offer of a chair and remained standing just inside the closed office door.

"Tell us about the night of the murder," Weston said.

"I already spoke to the police about this."

"Oh? And what did they say when you told them LeBlanc's killer gave you a message to pass along?"

Barnstead shared an uneasy glance with Hamilton. It was fleeting but clear. "I... I didn't tell them about that."

"Why not?" Kate asked.

Again Barnstead shot a questioning look at her boss. Hamilton hesitated before offering a reluctant nod in return, and Barnstead started talking.

"He specifically said not to tell them about it. He said if I told them *anything* about his message, or about the people it was meant for, he would come back and do to everyone here what he did to Peter. He said he would know if I told the police, and I believe him. So no, I didn't tell them."

She raised her head in a show of defiance.

"Who did he say you were to pass the message along to?" Weston asked.

"He said we'd be visited by a man and a woman, likely traveling with a physically challenged young boy. He said the visit would occur anywhere from a couple of days to a few weeks later, depending, as he put it, on how much attention you were paying."

Kate felt a black dread falling over her, a knot in her stomach that might explode into a radioactive blast at any moment.

"And what was this message?" she asked slowly, not wanting to hear the answer but knowing there was no way to avoid it.

"That you will never catch him. That he is smarter than you, and faster, and more deadly. That he has been killing longer than you can possibly imagine, much longer, and he has beaten better pursuers than you. That he will never stop."

Tears were rolling down Barnstead's face, and Hamilton's was chalk-white. Kate swallowed heavily and glanced at Weston, who showed no reaction.

She cleared her throat and said, "You recited that message with no hesitation whatsoever, Ms. Barnstead."

A trembling smile appeared on the young woman's face and then vanished. "He had the entire thing written out on a sheet of paper, and forced me to memorize it. I had to read it to him, over and over, while he tattooed the children. By the time he was done I knew it forward and backward."

"Do you still have that sheet of paper?" Weston asked.

She shook her head. "He took it with him."

Christopher's voice filled Kate's head.

You know what this means, don't you? That murder was meant for us. The Beast wants us in Brunswick.

Kate and Weston turned to look at Christopher, who continued rocking gently in his chair. He appeared to be a million miles away but clearly was not.

Kate found herself nodding in agreement and hoped neither of the two women had noticed, but they were both lost in their grief, fear, and confusion. It would take a lot more than a brief nod to get their attention.

"Tell us about the tattoos," Weston said to Barnstead.

She sniffled. "It was awful. The children were confused and crying. They didn't understand what was happening, and how could we explain it to them? The scene was near chaos when I arrived, I—"

"What do you mean when you arrived?" Hamilton blurted out. "My understanding was that the man didn't show up until well after your shift started."

Barnstead dropped her gaze and stared at the tops of her shoes. "I got here late that evening—I had car trouble and when I called Peter, he told me to take my time, that things were going smoothly and he could handle the children by himself for a couple of hours."

"That's in direct violation of policy," Hamilton said. "There should always be two staff members present when the children are awake."

Kate wanted to tell Hamilton what she could do with her policy. The violation was an issue for another day, especially when they were finally getting somewhere.

She pursed her lips and said, "Please continue, Ms. Barnstead."

Barnstead glanced apologetically at her stone-faced boss before continuing. "Anyway, by the time I got here, that animal had already begun tattooing. The children were crying, a couple of them were screaming, and poor Peter was beside himself, afraid one of them might be killed. It was horrible."

"What about your cell phone? Why didn't you call for help when you saw what was happening?"

She shook her head miserably. "If I'd acted quickly enough, I could have done exactly that. But I wandered into the multipurpose room and before I even realized what was going on, the man pointed a gun at my face and told me to hand over my phone."

Kate nodded and changed the subject again. Keeping a witness off-balance often led to the most honest—and revealing—answers. And surprise often worked in your favor.

"How did Dani Melanson escape that night?"

Barnstead's brows shot up. "Dani? How do you know Dani?"

"Never mind that. How did she escape?"

Once again, Barnstead glanced at her boss. This time her look was one of utter confusion. "I don't understand the question. Dani wasn't here."

"Wrong," Weston said. "She was here and she has the wrist tattoo to prove it."

Barnstead eyed him in disbelief. "That can't be right. All I saw were Peter and the kids. "

"Then maybe she escaped before you arrived," Kate said.

"LeBlanc didn't tell you about her?"

"He didn't say much of anything. He *couldn't*. The creep threatened to shoot us if we spoke."

Hamilton's face was pale. "If Dani was here, where is she now? You don't think that man—"

"She's perfectly fine," Weston said. "You don't need to worry about her, she's safe."

Both women gaped at him, then Hamilton frowned. "How could you know that? Who *are* you people?"

"That doesn't matter. But you can believe me when I tell you she's fine."

Neither woman seemed particularly comforted by the words. They didn't know their visitors from Adam and associated them with what had to be the worst trauma they'd ever experienced.

Kate gave Hamilton a flat cop stare. "So the police have no idea a potentially critical eyewitness was even here?"

"How would they? *We* didn't even know until just now."

"Then tell us about the man," Weston said to Barnstead. "What did he look like?"

"He was big. Very big. And he was ugly and intimidating."

"Specifically," Kate pressed. "Height? Weight? Hair color? Identifying marks? Anything you can think of would be helpful."

"I can't really be any more specific. It was all kind of a blur. To be honest, I'm not even sure I would recognize him again if I saw him on the street."

Kate sat back and sighed. Livvie Barnstead's words were almost exactly the same as Dani's. A man points a gun at a grown woman's face and she can't remember a single detail of his appearance? Not one?

I told you before, Chris said. *He makes them forget.*

Weston was asking another question of Barnstead, but it faded into the background as Kate concentrated on Christopher's comment. *Is he using mind control?*

I don't know, but would it be that hard to believe?

No, Kate decided, it wouldn't be hard to believe at all.

After they finished questioning Barnstead and the door shut

behind her, Hamilton seemed to have regained a bit of her fire.

"All right, we've answered your questions. Now, who *are* you two and how do you know Dani Melanson?"

"I already told you," Weston said, his voice steely. "That's not important."

"It's important to me. I've known that girl for a long time."

"You were told to expect us," Kate said. "So isn't it obvious we've had some experience with this guy?"

Hamilton huffed. "For all I know you're *working* with him."

"To do what? He's already done his damage. How could you possibly think we'd be part of something like that?"

"At this point I'm not sure what to think."

"Look," Kate said. "In one way or another, all three of us have been victimized by this freak. Just like LeBlanc, and just like those kids. And that's why we're here. But Dani is safe, and we aim to keep her safe. I'm sorry I can't offer you any more than that, but you'll just have to trust in our assurances."

Hamilton opened her mouth to argue but before she could, Weston said, "Or you could notify the police. Of course, then you'd have to explain how a thirteen-year-old girl—a material witness to a murder—disappeared from your facility without anyone knowing. I'm sure they'd be interested in hearing your explanation for that."

He glared at Hamilton, his eyes hard and unyielding, and after a moment's attempted defiance, she dropped her gaze. "I just wanted to be sure she was safe."

"We understand that," Kate said. "But what we *don't* understand is why she was here in the first place. We know about her brother, but isn't it unusual for a family member to be visiting for an entire week?"

Hamilton removed her glasses and dropped them onto her desktop with a clatter. She ran a hand over her face and for the first time Kate realized how haggard she looked, how exhausted. Her eyes were red-rimmed and wet.

"That poor child doesn't come from the best family situation," she said. "Father's an alcoholic, can't hold a job, mother's morbidly obese, unable to work and not interested in child rearing. Billy is two years older, but Family Services determined the parents were unable to provide him proper care."

"How long ago was that?"

"Almost three years. Dani is *extremely* close to the boy, and fiercely protective, and despite the fact that she's younger—she was only ten when Billy was removed from the home—she had long since taken on the role of protector for him."

"She acted as big sister."

"More like a mother than a sister, I would say. I don't think it would be possible to overstate how much those two children mean to each other. And once we realized how close they were, and given what we know about the family situation, we made the effort to allow Dani to spend as much time here with her brother as reasonably possible. This facility is quite large for the number of residents and staff currently occupying it, so we set up a vacant room for her. When she's not in school, she spends much of her time here."

"Okay," Kate said. "Then how could she disappear and be gone for three full days and nobody realize she's missing?"

"Because she comes and goes as she pleases. That's always been the arrangement. And I'm ashamed to admit this, but we have no established record-keeping to track when she's here and when she's not. She's not an official resident, so we've never needed to worry about it."

Kate shook her head. "What about your precious policy or state regulations? What about insurance? Surely having a child here who isn't a client is a potential liability."

Hamilton lowered her face into her hands. "Nobody knows about her. Not the state regulators, not our insurance carrier. Nobody. We just wanted to do the right thing for the girl and her brother. That's all. Our residents aren't violent, so there was no reason to believe Dani would be in any—"

A curt rap sounded on the office door, and three heads looked up simultaneously as Christopher continued to rock in his chair, seemingly oblivious.

On the other side of the wire-reinforced window stood a large middle-aged man in a dark blue suit, tie loosened, expression sour.

Everything in his manner screamed *cop.*

Kate looked back at Hamilton, who was frozen behind her desk, her eyes wide.

"Oh, god..." Hamilton said.

14

For a long moment nobody moved, and then the man knocked again and opened the door.

"May I help you?" Hamilton's voice shook and her face was chalk-white and Kate thought the offer of help might be the least sincere she'd heard since her last visit to a fast-food restaurant.

The man stepped through the doorway.

"I'm Detective Bannerman with Brunswick Homicide." His voice was cold and hard. He opened his suit jacket to reveal a gold shield clipped to his belt before letting the jacket drop back into place. "I'm here for some follow-up questions about Peter LeBlanc. I know you already spoke to one of my colleagues, but I wasn't on duty the night of the murder, and wanted to touch base with you myself."

Hamilton had regained a little of her composure—was no longer visibly shaking anyway—and she offered him an insincere little smile.

"Well, Detective, as you can see, I'm in the middle of something at the moment. This family is here for a tour of our facility."

Bannerman turned to examine the three of them curiously. His eyes glittered brightly and his presence made Kate uncomfortable, although she couldn't have said specifically why.

"That may be so," he said, "but this is a homicide investigation, and too much time has already passed since Mr. LeBlanc's murder. I need answers and I need them now."

The cop continued to stare at them.

After a career in law enforcement, the last thing Kate should feel in this man's presence was intimidation, but her discomfort had not dissipated. And she knew exactly what he would be thinking.

He would wonder exactly what Hamilton had wondered: what a family with a special needs child would be doing here four days after a brutal murder.

He would be wondering whether they read the newspaper or watched the news on TV or the Internet.

He would be wondering whether they were here for some other reason entirely.

All of this went through her head in roughly half a second as the inexplicable discomfort continued to build. Sweat formed in her armpits and her stomach started doing flip-flops.

She wanted Christopher's input.

Chris, are you getting anything from this guy?

No response.

It's like he's radiating some kind of... malevolence. Can you feel what I feel?

Still no response.

Chris?

He was gone. Physically, he was still seated on the chair next to her, rocking gently, face tilted up toward the ceiling. But mentally, he was gone.

As Detective Bannerman's gaze flitted from Hamilton to her guests and back, his forehead wrinkled and his cold eyes narrowed. Kate reluctantly arrived at the only conclusion she could: this situation was out of her control.

It was not a comforting realization.

She dropped her gaze to the dingy linoleum as she worked through the issue, then looked up to find Bannerman now staring directly at her, his eyes shrewd and focused.

Kate felt a drop of sweat trickle down the back of her neck and under her collar.

Bannerman pursed his lips. "Is there something you'd like to say, Ms...?"

He seemed to recognize the effect he was having on her.

He seemed to relish it.

"Karlson," she answered automatically. "Kate Karlson, and no, I have nothing to say."

"Because I could find a nice, quiet spot to chat if you'd like. Or I'm sure Ms. Hamilton would have no problem vacating her office for a few minutes if you want to talk in private."

The question only confirmed Kate's instincts about his thought process. The color that had returned to Hamilton's face now drained out again. Her eyes widened and she stared helplessly at Kate.

Kate realized there was no way this woman—terrified and guileless as she was—would be able to keep the secret of the Beast's message—and everything that went with it—for much longer. It was something of a miracle she hadn't folded already, a testament more to the power of the Beast's threats than to any intestinal fortitude the woman might possess.

But, threats or no threats, Hamilton would soon crumble, and the police would learn the truth. And if the three of them were around when that happened, they would find themselves occupying separate interrogation rooms, facing questions they couldn't answer, at least not to the satisfaction of a hard case like Bannerman.

That was a scenario they couldn't afford.

Kate locked eyes with the man.

Started to speak.

But before she could, Weston said, "We really don't know what you're talking about, Detective. I'm sorry to hear there was a murder here, but all we wanted was a tour of this facility, not to get caught up in a police investigation. So maybe you could turn around and walk back out that door and give us a few minutes to finish our business."

Bannerman's eyes widened almost comically, but the look in them was anything but humorous. It was exactly the opposite. It was the look of a man doing everything in his power to control his anger.

Finally he nodded slowly, his flinty gaze flitting from Weston to Kate before turning to Hamilton.

"Tell you what. I'll run into town and grab a coffee. I trust when I return, you'll have a moment to spare for me?"

"Of course," Hamilton said, but it was obvious to Kate the

woman wanted nothing to do with him. And if it was obvious to her, it had to be obvious to Bannerman as well.

"Fine," he said after a moment. "I'll be back in... oh, say, an hour. I look forward to chatting with you."

He stood at the door a moment longer, meeting the gaze of each of the adults, and then made a point of focusing on Christopher for a moment as well. The boy continued to rock, his unseeing gaze fixed on the ceiling.

Bannerman studied him with interest, then turned on his heel and was gone.

Hamilton maintained her composure for perhaps fifteen seconds after Detective Bannerman's footsteps had echoed away. Then she placed her elbows on her desk and lowered her head into her hands.

"Please," she said, her words floating out from around her fingers. "You have to tell me the truth. Why would that horrible man go to all the trouble of forcing Livvie to memorize a message meant for you? And how would he even know you'd show up?"

"There's nothing more to tell," Weston said.

"Just that you've all been victimized by him."

"That's right."

"Then why did his message make it sound like you're chasing him? Is that what you're holding back? You're out for what? Vengeance?"

Weston glanced at Kate. "Something like that."

Hamilton raised her head from her hands. Her eyes were watery and her exhaustion manifested itself in dark circles beneath them. "Seems to me it's *exactly* like that."

"Our motivations are irrelevant."

"Irrelevant?" Her tone was incredulous. "Your motivations are irrelevant? Excuse me, but they couldn't be *more* relevant! This man, this... this *monster*, killed one of my staff members in cold blood. He permanently disfigured a dozen children, most of whom could not even comprehend what was happening to them. He threatened violent death to Livvie and me and everyone else inside this facility, and after all of that you have the nerve to say your motivations are *irrelevant?*"

"We didn't have anything to do with—"

"Of course you did! You had everything to do with what happened here! Contrary to what you obviously believe, I'm not stupid. All of this was done with you in mind. All of it. Its sole purpose was to draw you here, so the killer could be sure you'd receive your damned message."

Hamilton was shaking now, her anger, fear, and confusion bubbling over after being bottled up for more than three days.

"This is all your fault, every last bit of it. And all I've done for three days is answer question after question from suspicious policemen while trying to figure out how in the world we're going to reassure our residents—and their families, not to mention the remainder of our living staff members—that they really are safe here. And I don't know how I can do that, because they aren't really safe here at all, and they never will be. None of us will ever be safe again."

"That's why we're trying to—"

"I don't care what you're trying to do and I'm sorry I even asked. I don't want to know anything *about* what you're trying to do. I've had it."

She ran a hand across her haggard face. When she spoke again, the hysterical tone in her voice was gone. Mostly. Instead it was cold and controlled.

"I've answered your questions. Livvie has passed along the man's message, the message that was so important it required all of this."

She lifted her arms and swept them in the general direction of the multipurpose room. "And now that it's all been done, I want nothing more to do with you. With any of you."

She focused her gaze on Christopher, who continued to rock quietly in his chair.

"I want you out of here and I don't ever want to see you again."

15

The short walk to the Rambler felt almost unreal, as if Kate had somehow received a full-body dose of Novocain. Numbness permeated every inch of her body, and even without speaking, she could tell Weston felt the same way. The glazed eyes and taut facial muscles were a dead giveaway.

Was it really possible a man was dead and more than a dozen innocent children permanently disfigured simply because a psychopath wanted to taunt them, to deliver a twisted message of superiority?

Could anyone be that sadistic?

Then Kate considered who they were dealing with. Of course the Beast could be that sadistic. It was perfectly in line with his personality to do such a thing. Any man capable of murdering innocent people, especially innocent children, and disfiguring their remains by slicing out their tongues could not be expected to observe normal behavioral boundaries.

Or *any* behavioral boundaries.

They approached the car without speaking. Kate opened the rear passenger door for Chris as Weston climbed behind the wheel. After she had the boy seated and belted, she slid in next to Weston and stared blankly ahead.

"That was... horrible."

"Which part?" Weston said. "The part where we learned this murder was staged specifically for us, or the part where psycho cop barged into the office and treated us like suspects?"

"So you think something was off about him, too?"

"How could I not? I'm not sure what Bannerman's deal is, but I don't find the fact that he's supposed to be one of the good guys particularly reassuring."

"Amen," Kate said. "And as far as the Beast goes, just because he took the opportunity to pass us a message after the killing doesn't mean he did it *because* of us. I'm not about to take the blame for his bullshit."

"Neither am I. But there's one thing we know for sure. This is the closest we've been to the freak since Alabama."

Kate nodded. "If Chris is right about him, we might be closer than even we realize. This is huge."

"Potentially, yes. I just wish Chris had been conscious for the whole meeting. If he hadn't been slipping in and out of the haze, he might have been able to pick up on something to help push us in the right direction. There obviously wasn't enough time for him to do a full gathering, especially with Bannerman nosing around, but anything would have been better than nothing."

Weston turned the key in the Rambler's ignition. The engine rumbled to life and he nudged the accelerator, backing out of their parking spot.

"So where do we go from here?" Kate asked.

"We need to question Dani again. I'm not buying this business about her being unable to give us a physical description of the Beast. The guy's face hung inches away from hers for however long it took him to ink her wrist."

"Except Barnstead couldn't describe him either. I don't know if you heard Chris and me, but we think the Beast might be using some kind of mind control."

Weston sighed and spun the wheel. "Something we can add to the list. But even if Dani can't remember every single detail of his appearance, she damn well has to know more than she's told us so far. And we have to find out what he said, if anything. Maybe he dropped some kind of a hint about what he's up to. Maybe he gave *her* a message, too."

Weston drove toward the wrought iron gate.

"After that," he continued, "after we wring every last bit of information we can out of that girl, we have to get her back to her home, and as soon as possible. I don't care what Chris has to say about it. If we're close to the Beast, then keeping her with us is only putting her in *more* danger, not less, and we don't need the responsibility of trying to protect another child when we already —"

It was him.

Weston stopped speaking as abruptly as if the words had been snipped in half with a pair of scissors. Despite all the months they'd spent with Chris, his emergence from the haze could never be predicted and always came without warning.

"*Who* was him?" Kate said. "What are you talking about?"

The detective. Bannerman. It was him.

The boy sounded weak and frightened. His words, normally strong and clear inside her head, seemed somehow clipped, cut-off, half-formed.

As if he was terrified.

"Chris, what are you saying?"

The Beast. He's the Beast. It's him.

The brakes squeaked as Weston brought the Rambler to a stop. "*Bannerman* is the Beast? That's not possible."

Why not?

"It just doesn't make any sense."

Because you wouldn't expect him to do something so rash? He always does the unexpected. We should know that by now. It was him.

Kate felt her scalp prickle. "Are you sure?"

I could feel him coming, getting closer, and the minute he opened that office door, I shut down. I couldn't control it, I couldn't help it.

He was almost in tears.

I'm sorry. When you needed me most I shut down.

"It's okay," Weston said, trying to soothe him.

Kate thought back to her uneasiness at Bannerman's arrival, to the utter lack of empathy in his manner, to the stone coldness in his words and expressions.

"But why?" she said. "Why would he do it? Why would he risk walking back into that place after everything he did, especially with Livvie Barnstead inside the facility? She could identify..."

Kate stopped herself, because, of course, that wasn't strictly true. If the Beast had used some kind of mind control, maybe even seeing him again would do nothing to jar Barnstead's memory.

Besides, Chris had no reason to lie, and while his powers were not infallible, the sheer terror and sensory overload from the close proximity of the man who had hacked out his tongue would explain the abrupt disappearance into his own head.

His circuits had shorted out.

And what about her own circuits? If push came to shove, could she herself describe Detective Bannerman? She was a trained investigator, schooled in the art of remembering details about perps and crime scenes. But now all she could see was *big. Ugly.*

The same words Dani and Livvie Barnstead had used.

She looked at Weston, who seemed to be struggling to work out an equation that was impossible to solve.

"Are you having the same problem I am?" she asked.

"If it has something to do with the words 'big' and 'ugly', then, yes, I am."

The car fell silent.

No big surprise there.

The question was why? Why had the Beast done this? Invading The Mission, killing Peter LeBlanc, forcing Livvie Barnstead to memorize that taunting message, and now returning to the scene of the crime—literally.

None of it made sense.

He's still close, Chris said into the looming silence. *He's very close. I can feel him.*

Weston stepped on the gas and the Rambler surged forward. "This makes questioning Dani even more time-critical. If *we* can't remember what the bastard looks like, she might be a lost cause. But we have to try to get every last bit of information out of her that we can."

Kate nodded. "I agree."

"Whatever's happening here isn't over yet. Killing LeBlanc and inking those kids was just the first act. And we're running out of time. I can feel it."

So can I.

PART TWO

"A man that does nothing but watch evil, never will overcome it."
                                                    ~Henry Ward Beecher

16

Dani was engrossed in her book when they walked into the motel room. She smiled and leapt off the bed at the sight of Christopher, and then crossed the room to the door and grabbed his hand.

Chris didn't need anyone's help navigating the furniture, but he allowed himself to be led to a chair at the writing table. He smiled and nodded as she whispered something into his ear.

After helping him into his chair, Dani looked up at Kate and Weston. "How did it go? Is my brother okay?"

Kate was embarrassed to realize she hadn't thought to find out which one of the kids actually *was* Dani's brother, but they'd all seemed in fairly good shape, considering the circumstances.

"He's good," she said. "They're all good."

Dani nodded. "I figured he would be, or I would've heard something about it on the news. But thank you for checking in on him."

Kate felt a stab of guilt. "No problem," she said.

"Can we go get lunch now? I'm starving."

"That can wait," Weston told her. "We need some answers. *Now.*"

Dani frowned. "What's wrong? Why are you yelling?"

"I'm not yelling. Not yet, at least. But we really need to talk."

"About what?"

"The Mission."

"I told you everything I know."

"You haven't told us anything yet. Nothing specific, anyway."

Dani's face reddened with anger. "What's that supposed to mean?"

Weston moved toward her. "You may not remember what he looked like, but I want to know every last word that man uttered to you while he was giving you that tattoo. If he belched, if he swore, if he asked someone what time it was, I want to know about it. Every last word."

"I already told you, I don't remember!"

Kate put her arm on Weston's. "Let's slow down a little."

Weston ignored her, taking another step toward Dani. "You expect me to believe that? I'm supposed to accept that you can't remember a single word he said? Nothing?"

"I told you everything I know!" She rose onto her tiptoes to bring her upturned face as close to Weston's as possible. "You can't yell at me, you're not my dad, even if you try to act like it. I don't care if you believe me or not. And I don't need you, I was doing just fine before you picked me up yesterday, and I can do just fine on my own."

She stomped across the room, angry eyes holding Weston's gaze the entire way. Then she opened the door.

Kate said, "Wait a second, Dani. Don't go. It's not safe."

"I know when I'm not wanted." Her eyes had filled with tears and now they spilled down her face. She stepped through the door and slammed it behind her.

What are you doing? We can't let her go.

Kate looked at Weston, who stood with the car keys dangling from his right hand.

Go, Chris said. *I'll be fine here by myself. Go get her.*

Dani was nowhere to be seen when they stepped outside. But she didn't have more than a thirty second head start on them, and even if she had taken off running, she couldn't have gotten far.

They climbed into the Rambler and started toward the road.

"Pick a direction," Weston said, his simmering anger still evident.

"Try going right," Kate told him, and as he spun the wheel, added, "What was that all about? Don't you think you were a little hard on the girl?"

"Maybe not hard enough."

"When I agreed we should question her again, I wasn't expecting you to go ballistic."

They were moving slow, Kate scanning the right side of the road, Weston the left.

"The guy was right in front of her, Kate, and she can't—or won't —give us a goddamn thing. He had to say *something* to her in all that time. He seemed to enjoy running his mouth in Hamilton's office."

"Maybe that was only for our benefit."

"I don't buy it. He's a talker."

"So what if he is? That doesn't mean she remembers anything he said. Do you?"

Weston shook his head. "Not verbatim, no. But it was all inconsequential bullshit designed to make us feel uncomfortable."

"So what makes you think it was any different for her?"

"I just need to know."

"Then tell me this: do you even remember what he sounded like?"

"What do you mean?"

"His voice. His accent. Because I don't know if he was a soprano or a deep baritone or if he came out of Boston or freaking Montreal. The truth is, if he walked up to us right now and started running his mouth, I wouldn't be able to tell you if it's the same guy."

Weston turned and stared at Kate, his mouth half-open. "Shit. He's a phantom. A complete phantom. For all we know, we could have interacted with him before."

Kate shivered at the thought.

"Don't even go there," she said. "The point is, even if he *did* say something to Dani, expecting her to remember it—unless he *wanted* her to—is no different than expecting her to describe what he looks like. She can't, and neither can we. And screaming at her was downright cruel."

Weston said nothing for a moment, then shot Kate a glance. "I really *do* hate it when you're right."

"Pull into that parking lot up the street."

"Why?"

Kate pointed to a figure standing in front of the entrance to a small coffee shop. "Because there she is."

Dani looked furious, her hands balled into fists and jammed against her hips. She glared at them as the Rambler eased to a stop.

Kate lowered the window, but before she could say a word, Dani waved a dismissive hand at her. "Just go away and leave me alone."

"Mr. Weston has something he wants to say to you. Would that be all right?"

"I don't *care* what he wants to say. Leave me alone!"

Weston set the parking brake, then popped his door open and climbed out, speaking to her over the top of the Rambler. "Dani, I owe you an apology. I'm sorry about how I came at you back at the motel."

"Yeah, I'll bet."

"I mean it. I was upset and had no right to take my frustration out on you. And I believe you when you say you've told us everything you can remember about that creep. Finding him is very important to us, and I allowed that to cloud my judgment."

She sniffled and pursed her lips, and at that moment looked every bit her age. She might have been streetwise, but she was still barely more than a child. A child who was now standing unprotected in a public place while the Beast roamed the streets of Brunswick.

"Climb into the car," Weston said. "Come back to the motel with us until we can get you home."

"You're not my father."

"I know that."

She hesitated, still unconvinced.

"Come on," Kate said, "Chris'll be very sad if you leave us without at least saying goodbye to him."

Kate felt another stab of guilt for manipulating her. But it was overshadowed by her concern for the girl's welfare. The Beast was near, and Christopher seemed convinced that Dani had a major role to play in whatever was happening in Brunswick. Until they could figure it out, they had to get her off the streets.

"Fine," Dani sighed, then trudged to the Rambler, opened the rear door, and slipped onto the back seat. "I didn't have any money for lunch, anyway." She grinned at Kate, her still-wet eyes suddenly shining. "Aren't you guys hungry?"

They ate for the second time in as many days at The Lobster Claw.

Dani repeated yesterday's exercise with Chris, leading him into the restaurant by the hand, completely at ease with him, talking and joking despite his inability to answer her.

The clock was ticking on their time with Dani Melanson. The line between "protection" and "kidnapping" was a blurry one, and she would have to be returned to her parents' care soon.

Still, it was clear by Weston's demeanor that despite what they now knew about the Beast, he held out hope that they might learn something more from the girl.

They ate at a leisurely pace, and as they chatted, Kate knew he was waiting for the opportunity to turn the subject back to the events of four nights ago.

Dani surprised her by doing it for him.

She cleared her throat. "Um... you told me you checked on Billy, but did you tell him I'm okay, too?"

Kate felt yet another stab of guilt. "The truth is, we didn't get a chance to speak to him specifically. They were all working on art projects when we saw them."

Dani nodded and Weston wasted no time taking advantage of the opportunity he had been given. "There's something I've been wondering about you and Billy."

The girl raised her eyebrows in an unspoken invitation to continue.

"Ms. Hamilton told us you're extremely close to him."

"He needs a lot of help, and... well... he doesn't get it from our mom and dad."

"I understand," Weston said. "But wasn't it hard to leave him at The Mission with that man there?"

Dani's eyes grew wide. "What are you saying?"

"I know you were scared. But you must've been scared for him, too."

"I was *really* scared for him and I didn't want to leave him, but I knew I had to do it anyway. Nobody knew that man was there, and I thought if I could get help, maybe I could stop him before he hurt anybody else. But then I got outside and got lost in the dark, and... and..."

Tears filled her eyes and Kate patted her hand.

"It's all right, Dani. You were probably in shock—probably still are to some degree—but at least you tried. And you did better than a lot of adults would have. You were incredibly brave."

"Let's go back to what the man did to you," Weston said. "You told us the kids were all gathered around you when you got that tattoo. And that none of them seemed to understand what was happening."

Dani wiped her face and shifted uncomfortably. "That's right."

"Ms. Barnstead painted a different picture about that night."

Dani frowned. "How would *she* know? She wasn't even there."

"She came after you were already gone. She said it was quite chaotic, with children crying and the counselors struggling to keep them under control."

"I guess that happened later, then. The others didn't understand what was going on when I was in the chair, but the first time one of them started getting stabbed with a needle, the picture got clear pretty fast."

The girl had stopped eating and Kate noticed she was trembling.

Weston drummed his fingers on the table. "I know you said you don't remember what this creep looked like," Dani's eyebrows narrowed and he hurriedly added, "and I believe you. But are you sure he didn't say anything while he was working that might help us figure out what he's doing here, or where he might show up next?"

Still trembling, she dropped her gaze to the tattoo on her arm, concentrating, thinking back to what had to be the most frightening moment of her life.

You're scaring her.

Chris sounded short-tempered and upset, and Kate knew she had to turn this conversation around in a hurry or it would be too late.

When Dani looked up again, Kate reached over and gently touched her arm again, which was still red and puffy where the Beast had defiled her. "I know what happened that night is awful to think about, but there's something I need to tell you."

Wide, frightened eyes stared back at her.

"Everyone at this table has been hurt by the man who did this to you. All of us. We know exactly how you feel. We're here because of that man and we're determined to make sure he never hurts anyone else ever again."

Dani swallowed heavily and heaved a shaky sigh. She shifted her attention to Weston. "He didn't really talk."

"Think hard," Weston prompted. "It might have seemed like nothing at the time, something totally innocent, maybe even nonsensical-sounding. Do you remember anything like that?"

She shook her head. "All I remember is him telling the counselors to keep the kids quiet, or for me to sit still, stuff like that. Maybe he talked more later, but by then I was long gone."

"I've been meaning to ask you about that," Kate said. "How did you manage to get out of there?"

"After he finished with my tattoo, he started putting this circle mark on one of the other kids. He wasn't paying much attention to me anymore, so I told him I needed to pee. I was a little surprised when he said I could."

Kate furrowed her brow as she considered Dani's words. "Wasn't he worried you'd simply run out the front door?"

"There was no reason for him to worry about that. The front door was upstairs and in the other direction, and he would have known right away if I turned toward the stairs. Besides, the doors are always locked. Only staff members have the key. I couldn't have gone out the front door even if I wanted to."

"But how would he know that?"

"I don't know, but he seemed kind of familiar with the way things operate. It was almost like he'd been there before."

Kate shared a glance with Weston and knew exactly what he was thinking: the Beast may not have been at The Mission before, but he sure as hell was familiar with the workings of a group home.

Then again maybe he *had* been there, only no one remembered it.

"Okay," she said. "So you told the man you needed to go to the bathroom. What then?"

Dani looked away and gnawed on her lip. "I don't wanna get in trouble."

"We're not here to get anybody in trouble," Kate said. "Especially you. We won't repeat a word of what you tell us. Not to anyone."

She wanted to add, "probably," but thought better of it.

"Okay," Dani said. "See, all of the windows are locked at The Mission. They have to be really careful with the residents, because they need a lot of help with even the simplest things."

"We understand."

"The way the windows are kept locked is by an iron bar that runs along the inside track thingie that the bottom window slides on when you push it up. You can raise the window a few inches to let in some air, but then the window frame runs into the bar and won't go any higher."

"So nobody can push the window high enough to allow them to crawl through."

"That's right," Dani said, nodding emphatically. "But, see, the bar is... kinda... *broken* on this window."

"Broken."

"Yeah."

"How is it broken?"

"I found out a while ago that if you stick something between the bar and the window frame and pry it up, the bar pops right out of the frame."

"So that's what you did that night."

"Yes, I hid a spoon in the bathroom months ago, after I found out I could open the window. So after I told the man I had to pee, I went into the bathroom and popped out the bar. I pushed up the window and crawled out. Then I ran like mad."

"I don't understand something," Weston said. "I get that the window made a good escape route, but Ms. Hamilton told us you're normally free to come and go as you please, so it wasn't like you had to sneak around or anything. How did you even find out the lock was broken?"

"That's only true during the day. About coming and going. If I decide to sleep over, they don't want me going outside at night. But it used to get boring there, so sometimes I would, you know, slip out the window and go downtown for a while."

Kate and Weston shared another glance and Dani immediately said, "You promised you wouldn't get me in trouble if I told you."

"We won't," Kate said, "but you must realize how dangerous it is for a girl your age to be wandering around downtown at night by yourself."

"It can't be any more dangerous than what happened to me at The Mission."

Kate realized she had no response.

17

Jane Hamilton had promised herself when she got up this morning that she would spend the entire day at the office. She hadn't been able to manage a full day since the murder, feeling tired and distracted. But with a job like hers, working a part-time schedule was a luxury she simply couldn't afford.

She had felt physically ill every day since learning of the intruder's unadulterated evil, and today was no different. Between thinking about what the man had done to poor Peter, seeing the awful tattoos inked into the wrists of the children, and the unending visits by the police, whose presence had constituted an intrusion of their own, she suspected she would feel sick to her stomach for the rest of her life.

She had done okay for a while today. The nausea lurked in the background, a persistent reminder that it could come roaring back at any time, but she had been able to concentrate for a change and actually get some real work done.

Then that couple had shown up with the boy.

The couple the intruder had told Livvie to expect.

And Livvie, of course, had relayed the information to *her*, as if doing so absolved her of any responsibility for its passage.

And even though the girl had been on duty during the couple's arrival—thank god for small favors—and the message had been passed along as instructed, Hamilton felt the familiar sick sensation returning.

Maybe it was because of that awful Detective Bannerman.

She had been uncomfortable with the presence of all the policemen who had trooped through the building over the last three days, but Bannerman represented the corrupted cherry on top of the sundae of horror she'd felt ever since receiving Livvie's panicked and desperate phone call.

She knew she should be grateful for their efforts to find and incarcerate Peter's killer, and in a general, theoretical sense she was. But generalities had a way of vanishing into thin air when faced with a man like Bannerman, whose every pore seemed to ooze with violence and barely restrained ill intent.

If *he* was one of the good guys, how thin was the line between him and the bad guys he was supposed to be hunting?

Hamilton shut her eyes and attempted to center herself, but felt as if the walls of her office were closing in on her.

Despite her previous determination to stick out the entire day, her resolve folded like a cheap tent in a windstorm. She was a big believer in knowing one's limitations, and the prospect of facing that big, ugly cop again—alone in her office this time—was simply more than she could bear.

Bannerman would undoubtedly be angry, but he would have to get over it. His questions could wait until tomorrow and if not, tough. Peter was dead and nothing the authorities could do would bring him back.

Hamilton powered down her computer, shoved her paperwork into the top drawer of her desk, and then hurried out of her office just minutes after the Karlson couple left.

She glanced at her watch. The children's arts and crafts project would have ended by now, but she knew everyone would still be in the multipurpose room, listening to one of the counselors read a story.

She pushed open the door and walked into the room, heels clicking on the decades-old linoleum floor.

She quickly found Livvie and pulled her aside. "I'm not feeling well. I'll be leaving early today. If there are any problems, please call my home phone."

Livvie gazed back at her and Hamilton felt a stab of shame. This girl was young, barely twenty, and had suffered much more than Hamilton had. She had been a direct witness to the horror, had been forced to watch as Peter was butchered and killed. She had then been faced with the unenviable task of keeping it together for the children, and Hamilton wondered how she managed.

The fact that she'd even come back to work was something of a miracle.

But Livvie was an hourly employee. A contractor, really, without the benefit of paid leave. She didn't have the option of going home simply because she was nervous, or upset, or afraid. If she chose to do so, not only would she lose half a day's pay, she'd put herself at risk of losing her job altogether.

Hamilton could run home with her tail between her legs, but Livvie would have to stick it out, regardless of how she might be feeling.

Still, despite her shame, Hamilton held her head high. She was in charge, and if she wanted—or needed—to go home early, that was her own business, and nobody else's.

"I understand," Livvie said, watching her steadily. "I'm sure we'll be fine."

Hamilton lowered her gaze and turned toward the door.

The man with the tattoo had been prepared to wait several more hours for Jane Hamilton to leave work. But after his Oscar-worthy performance as Detective Bannerman, he wasn't the least bit surprised to see her drive out of the lot less than fifteen minutes after the departure of his friends in the old white station wagon.

He'd scared the shit out of that fat fucking bitch.

But then instilling fear was his bread and butter. He had been doing it longer than he cared to think about, and by now he could tell, without question, when he had been successful.

And Hamilton was success personified.

He wasn't as sure about his friends, however. Oh, he'd frightened them all right, but to what degree? Certainly not as deeply and irrevocably as he'd frightened the bitch. But then the three of them had already been exposed—and hardened—to his particular brand of fun. And while his little exercise in smoke and mirrors was bound to have unsettled them somewhat, he doubted it would weaken their resolve.

If it did, what good were they? Their determination to shut him down was the fuel that propelled him.

Not that it mattered right now. Hamilton had been the target today. Mind fucking the other three was nothing more than a side benefit.

A pleasing corollary.

After stalking out of the fat bitch's office, he had hurried back to his car, still parked in his surveillance spot, and prepared for the inevitable next act in this elaborately constructed play.

Now he straightened his tie and ran his fingers over the detective's shield clipped to his belt—one he'd taken from an actual cop just two months ago, after slitting his throat (no time to take his tongue, unfortunately)—and watched as her dark sedan approached The Mission's front gate.

After grabbing his trusty binoculars, he trained them on the interior of the car. The angle gave him a clear view, and unless someone was lying on the floor, Hamilton was the only occupant.

That was very good news for the man with the tattoo.

He waited a moment, then started his engine and followed.

Just parking in the driveway and walking into the house made Hamilton feel better. Only marginally so, but still, at this point she was willing to take whatever she could get.

Tomorrow she would definitely spend the entire day at work. No question about it. Maybe she would even stay late to catch up on a few things. With the exception of her meeting with what was sure to be an angry and unpleasant Detective Bannerman, the worst of this ordeal was over. The police were no longer swarming all over the facility, the message from the lunatic had been delivered to the young couple, and the killer was surely by now dozens of states away.

Tomorrow, things would almost certainly begin to look better.

Today, though, it was just a relief to be home. Jane kicked her heels off inside the door and walked to her wine rack. Removed a bottle of Pinot and poured a nice, tall glass. Not a wine glass, either. A water tumbler.

A wine glass wasn't going to cut it today.

She had just settled onto her couch when the doorbell rang. She gasped and her whole body jerked reflexively and she damned near spilled wine down the front of her blouse. Her nerves were strung as tight as guitar strings.

Who the hell could *this* be?

She craned her neck and looked out the front window. A nondescript sedan was parked behind her car, but the vehicle was empty, which made sense, since *someone* had to have rung the bell.

She blew out a breath in frustration—it sounded shaky, no surprise there—and pushed herself to her feet. Crossed the living room and reached for the door.

Then she pulled her hand back as if she had just been hit with an electric shock. Up until three days ago she would have yanked it open without giving it a second thought, but not anymore.

Brunswick born and raised, Hamilton had always viewed her hometown as quiet and sleepy, safe. Now she realized there was no such thing as "safe." The concept was nothing more than a delusion. One we sold ourselves as human beings to allow us to get through the day without suffering a total breakdown.

Evil was everywhere. It could appear at any time, with no warning.

The doorbell rang a second time and her body jerked again.

"Christ, get ahold of yourself," she muttered before hollering, "Who is it?" in the angriest voice she could muster.

"Detective Bannerman. Have you forgotten our appointment already?"

The voice floated through the door like that of a ghost. A malignant, curt, belligerent ghost.

Instantly, Hamilton started shaking. Her fear skyrocketed, exactly as it had when she'd first seen Bannerman back at The Mission. She had been a fool to think things were beginning to improve. She should have known better.

"Ms. Hamilton, I'm waiting."

Bile rushed up into her mouth and she choked it back.

Then she swung open the door.

18

The look on the fat bitch's face was priceless.

The man with the tattoo wished he could preserve this moment forever, maybe whip out a cell phone and snap a quick pic or two.

But time was passing, and things would proceed much more smoothly if he took advantage of the fact that the woman had been shocked into inaction. Her surprise would only last for a second or two, and at the moment she was frozen in place like a fucking statue.

So he committed her expression to memory, determined to enjoy it more fully later. Then he smiled broadly and pushed his way into the foyer.

"Hello, Jane," he said, swinging the front door closed. "Long time no see. Miss me?"

"Uh... D-Detective Bannerman... I...I..."

"That's a nasty little stutter you've got there. Funny I didn't notice it before. You weren't trying to skip out on me, were you?"

The bitch gaped at him open-mouthed and said nothing.

He leaned in close to her now, whispering into her ear. "Don't tell anyone, but I'm gonna let you in on a little secret. Bannerman isn't my real name and detecting is definitely not my game. At least not in the typical sense."

Hamilton didn't move. Seemed incapable of it.

"You see," he continued, "the reason I'm telling you this is because we're about to get to know each other very... intimately. So, it only makes sense that we break down the barriers between us. Don't you agree?"

She stank of fear and was breathing hard now. As if she had just sprinted the length of a football field, something she probably hadn't done in decades, if ever. Not in her fat-ass condition. The color had drained out of her face and she looked as though she might faint dead away.

That would be counterproductive. He needed information and although he was perfectly comfortable waiting here for it if necessary, there was no reason to delay things, either, when the proper approach should yield quick results.

"Don't worry," he soothed. "I don't mean to imply intimacy in the commonly understood sense. Nothing sexual will happen here today, of that you can rest assured. What I mean by 'intimacy' is something a little less... conventional. But we'll get to that later, all right, Jane?"

She took in a deep breath and opened her mouth and he knew a scream would soon follow.

That would not be good. This was a quiet neighborhood, and even though most people would still be at work at this time of day —not everyone could afford to slack off like Jane Hamilton—undoubtedly *someone* would be home within hearing distance, and that someone would likely not allow a scream to go uninvestigated.

"I strongly suggest you reconsider what you're about to do," he said, his voice low and smooth and deadly. "If you scream, or if you attempt to run, or if you do anything at all to draw attention to the two of us and our little impromptu meeting of the minds, the consequences will be... severe. You will most assuredly *not* enjoy what will follow. Do we understand each other, Jane?"

The woman's eyes widened but her mouth snapped closed, and while she didn't answer, she also didn't scream.

One small victory.

"Now," he said. "Let's go into your living room and chat like civilized human beings, shall we?"

He took her by the elbow and steered her toward the couch. Spotted her glass, filled to the brim with red wine and said, "Getting an early start on Happy Hour, I see."

She glanced from his face to the glass and said nothing.

"I don't blame you. It's been a rough week, hasn't it? But I have no problem if you drink while we continue our conversation.

Although, in strict grammatical terms, calling what's taken place so far a 'conversation' would be a stretch. Except for a stutter or two, you've been remiss in holding up your end of the bargain."

He shoved her onto the couch and loomed over her.

"So, please... take a generous sip of your wine. Maybe a few. It should help loosen your tongue. And before you *lose* that tongue, there are some things I need to know."

"I—I—I..."

"There it is again. Try to speak in complete sentences, please."

The bitch took a nervous gulp of her wine to steel herself. And lo and behold, it actually seemed to work, although her voice shook when she spoke.

"I'm... sorry about leaving before your return this afternoon."

He waved one hand airily. "I expected no less. In fact, you did exactly what I wanted you to do by running home. There wasn't nearly enough privacy in that shitty little box you call an office. Not for what I have in mind."

She gaped at him uncomprehendingly and he continued.

"Really, Jane, you helped me out immensely, dealing with my three friends the way you did, making sure your girl Livvie gave them my message. And it does a heart good to discover there are still at least a few outliers in this world who can be trusted, don't you think? So many people these days are all about themselves, and what *they* want, and what *they* need, and the hell with everyone else."

The bitch stared at him, slack-jawed.

"Don't you agree?" he barked, spitting the words out sharply.

"I... I... yes, I agree," she said. "Of course I agree."

Her voice shook again and cracked and she stared dumbly down at her crotch, where the material of her slacks was darkening.

Oh, joy.

She was pissing herself.

Terror was a wonderful motivator, the best, really, as long as she didn't become so frightened her fucking heart stopped. That would happen soon enough, but it would be a real tragedy if her ticker quit working before he got what he came here for.

It was time to pick up the pace.

"I have to be honest, " he said. "I hadn't really planned on this tete-a-tete. But when I came to visit you today, I discovered something that caught me completely by surprise, and I hope you don't think I'm being boastful when I tell you I'm not easily surprised."

She gulped down another mouthful of wine. Her hands were shaking and it sloshed out of the tumbler, splattering the front of her blouse and dripping down her face. She glanced at him from over the rim of the glass, which she clutched with almost religious fervor in front of her eyes as though it might somehow protect her from what was to come.

It would not. But if it helped her get through the next few minutes, he had no problem with that.

She stared at him now, eyes glazed, and he decided to take that as acknowledgment that, no, she didn't consider him boastful.

"Anyway, that's what drew me here today. When I came to visit you and my three amigos, I discovered they had somehow managed to meet up with someone unexpected when they arrived in your little shitberg. Someone you know."

The woman shook her head dumbly. It was clear she had no idea who he was talking about.

But he'd expected that. The girl hadn't been with them during their visit to The Mission, so Hamilton—unless blessed with abilities similar to his own, a possibility that was unlikely in the extreme—would have no way of knowing they'd been in contact with her.

And *he* only knew because of the boy.

He could smell the girl on him. Smell her fear. Radiating off the little bastard just as it had radiated off *her* when he'd given her that pretty new tattoo.

And the boy cared about her. That was the exquisite thing. That was what made this meeting so important.

The fact that she was no longer with them suggested they had done the right thing, the saintly thing, and taken her home to mommy and daddy where she would be safe in their loving arms. That would also mean the police would eventually be called, but this was of less concern to him than actually finding the girl.

Which left him in a bit of a quandary, because he didn't even know her name.

"This brings us to the point of our little chat. And again, I hesitate to label it a 'conversation.' So far. For your sake, I hope that changes soon."

"What do you want to know?" she croaked. The words came out gruff and scratchy, but clear.

He smiled. The slack expression on her face had been cause for concern, but obviously she was paying attention, which meant he should be able to get what he needed from her.

"I want the name of the young girl whose brother is a resident of The Mission."

She stared.

"Come now, Jane, you know who I mean. She's in her early teens, going to be very beautiful, and she spends a lot of her time in that shit hole because her brother resides there. She was there the other night, in fact, although in all the excitement of my whirlwind visit, I have to admit I had forgotten all about her until I... sensed her... earlier today."

"Why... why do you want to know who she is?"

"Because finding her would be nearly impossible *without* that information, even in a city as small and isolated as Brunswick."

"But... *why* do you want to find her? What could you possibly want with her?" The woman's hands were shaking even more now, and the thought occurred to him that if she didn't get herself under control, her glass would soon be empty, and not because she had drunk it all.

The notion struck him as humorous, but as tempting as it was to see if he could get the old lady to spill the remainder of her wine all over herself, time was ticking. And if he was going to accomplish what he so badly wanted—to send a *second* message to the boy and his two worthless lap dogs, one that would truly hammer home his superiority over them—playing silly games would be counterproductive.

He smiled without any hint of friendliness. "It's not any of your business what I want with her. I've already asked you her name once, and I rarely offer people who displease me a second chance. But since we haven't gotten to know each other very well—yet—I will ask you one more time. If you then choose not to answer, things will become... unnecessarily unpleasant for you."

She moaned miserably and he said, "Tell me her name."

"Dani Melanson. Her name is Dani Melanson. Her brother's name is—"

"You can stop right there. I don't give a flying fuck about her brother. I care about her. Where does she live?"

"I-I don't know. I have all of that information on file, of course, back at the office. I could go retrieve it if you'd like, it wouldn't take long. I can just get right in my car and drive to the office and —"

"Enough."

The bitch recoiled. Her desperate attempt to stall, to delay the inevitable, was as obvious as it was pathetic, and he had little tolerance for sniveling. Now, thanks to her babbling, he was running out of patience as well as time.

"Forget the address. Just tell me the names of her mommy and daddy. That's all I need."

She opened and closed her mouth a couple times, then said, "Thomas and Maureen Melanson."

The man with the tattoo took one step forward and the woman shrank back into the couch. If she could force herself between the cushions he had no doubt she would. But she could not, of course, and he came to a stop directly in front of her. She dropped her nearly empty tumbler of wine and it bounced off her knee and fell to the carpeted floor at her feet.

He paid no attention to it.

"Thank you for your cooperation," he said softly. "Young Dani is of critical importance to me. More important to me than I'm sure you realize. But don't feel bad. Even I didn't recognize the role she has to play in this little drama until this morning, and I'm the one pulling the strings. And now that you've given me what I need, we're left with a problem. It's a fairly significant problem, too, especially for you. Do you know what that problem is, Jane?"

It was almost as though she didn't even hear his words. She

stared into his eyes, her face white as a sheet, her lips pale. It seemed obvious what the problem was, and he assumed that if she weren't so stressed she would recognize it immediately.

But time was an issue, so he decided to fill in the blanks for her. "I can't trust you not to go to the police after I leave here. Not that it matters all that much. You wouldn't be able to describe me to them or tell them what we've talked about. But I can't reasonably expect you to keep secret this encounter, as personal and intimate as it's been and is yet to be. And if word of it were to somehow trickle down to my three friends, well, all the fun I have planned for them would be ruined. So while I very much appreciate your assistance, I'm afraid we need to draw our time together to a conclusion."

He flashed another smile as he reached into his back pocket for his utility knife. "A permanent one."

He waited for a response but didn't receive one. He doubted the bitch had even understood his words. She was too far gone now, sobbing, tears rolling down her face and snot bubbling out of one nostril.

It was disgusting.

He crouched down in front of her, flicking the knife open with a *snick.*

"Do me a favor, would you? Open wide and say 'ahhh.'"

19

Depot Road in Lisbon was old. It was also narrow and winding and badly in need of maintenance. Potholes scattered along the pavement made it nearly impossible for Weston to coax much more than twenty miles per hour out of the Rambler without shearing off an axle.

The farther they drove, the thicker the trees and underbrush seemed to get, blotting out the daylight, leaving them surrounded by a fuzzy grey murkiness, as if night were falling in the middle of the afternoon. The shadows seemed appropriate to Kate's mood.

Gentle questioning of Dani as they drove had revealed that after escaping The Mission, the girl's plan—if you could call it that—had been to hike all the way to Lisbon. But fear of the man who had tattooed her prevented her from walking along the road, and once into the woods, under dark, cloud-covered skies, she had become hopelessly lost.

After two full days and part of a third spent wandering in the forest northwest of Brunswick, she had finally found her way back to the city, feeling tired, dirty and hungry. She emerged less than a mile from The Mission and was picked up almost immediately by Kate, Weston and Chris.

The girl's story chilled Kate, particularly the dispassionate way she related it, as if she were doing nothing more than describing what she had eaten for dinner last night. It was clear she was trying to keep herself together, and although prior to coming to Maine, Kate had doubted she could ever hate the Beast more than she already did, she was beginning to discover she had been wrong about that.

They encountered no traffic on Depot Road as they drove, and few homes interrupted the nearly unbroken wilderness in this portion of central Maine. At last they rounded a sharp corner, the road taking a turn of nearly ninety degrees for no discernible reason, and Dani pointed through the windshield.

"That's it. Up ahead on the right."

At first, Kate couldn't tell what the girl was pointing at. To her eyes, the trees and brush crowding the road remained unbroken, but as Weston approached the area, a narrow opening resolved itself and he turned off Depot Road.

A driveway that at one time had been gravel but now was mostly just a thick row of weeds separated by two rutted tracks wound toward a decrepit house trailer perched precariously on a foundation of concrete blocks. A Ford F-150 pickup that had to be twenty-five years old was parked at an angle in front of the home, and off to the side and slightly behind the trailer a swing set sat rusting away. One of the chains had snapped, and a swing lay on its side on the ground, forgotten, scrub grass and weeds growing over and around it.

"Does the truck in the driveway mean your dad is home?" Kate asked.

Dani raised her eyes from her book and nodded.

"Are you excited to see him?"

She shrugged. "He's probably drunk or sleeping."

Kate shared a glance with Weston, thinking they should back out of the driveway right now and head away from this place as fast as they could. Take the girl to the Brunswick Police Department instead.

Or back to The Mission.

Or anywhere but here.

Apparently, Christopher felt the same way. He had been registering his disapproval of this plan on and off throughout the day, and now he tried again.

This is a mistake.

There's nothing we can do about it, Kate told him. *We can't keep her with us forever, and she should be plenty far away from the Beast way out here in the middle of nowhere.*

Kate believed it, too. And there was another consideration. She thought back to Weston's words from yesterday, spoken as they were driving into the city.

We're not here to save the world.

It was true. The odds of them being able to make any difference in Dani Melanson's life were minuscule, and even if they could, that difference would come at the cost of a lot of time, time they simply did not have if they wanted to stand any chance of running down the Beast before once again losing his trail.

And losing his trail would mean waiting helplessly for more innocents to be slaughtered.

As options went, that one was unacceptable. Dani's home life was clearly not ideal, but she had survived to this point to become a beautiful young woman, smart and independent and clearly loyal to her brother. She would only have to survive a few more years and then she would be on her own and away from here anyway.

Weston pulled to a stop behind the pickup and killed the engine. Dust swirled around the car in dwindling eddies. Their approach had not been quiet, as the Rambler's engine growled and the heavy car bounced and jolted along the poorly maintained driveway, but outside the windshield nothing moved.

Nobody opened the trailer's flimsy screen door.

No face appeared at any of the open windows.

The home was still and silent. It appeared empty. Abandoned.

Kate and Weston shared another glance and Kate turned to face the back seat. "I see the truck, but are you sure anyone's here?"

Dani sighed and dog-eared a page of her book. After closing the cover, she looked up again and shrugged. "I told you, my dad's probably drunk or sleeping." She was clearly not overcome with pleasure to be home, and Kate couldn't blame her.

"What about your mom?"

"What about her? She'll be doing what she always does. A big bunch of nothing."

Forcing a smile, Kate said, "Let's go, kiddo, I'll walk you to your door."

"That's okay," she said. "I'll be fine."

She had tears in her eyes as she turned to Chris and squeezed his arm, murmuring a soft "goodbye," then stepped out of the car and began trudging toward the trailer, head down.

Kate opened her door and Weston reached for his, saying, "Wait for Chris and me."

Kate shook her head. "I'll take care of this."

Weston nodded and Kate climbed out of the car, then caught up with Dani and fell into step beside her.

"I want to talk to one of your parents for a minute."

Not a puff of a breeze disturbed the stillness, and the air felt heavy, thick. A storm was coming. Kate could feel it in her bones, and in the headache forming at the base of her skull.

"You don't have to talk to anyone," Dani said in a voice that was half whine and half plea. "You've been trying to get me here since yesterday. Now that you've done it, just leave me alone!"

Kate ignored her and walked on. Her stomach was doing flip-flops and she didn't know why. They reached the trailer and Dani yanked on the screen door and it opened with a pained screech.

"Leave me *alone*," she repeated, her voice barely above a whisper.

"Not gonna happen," Kate said and followed her inside.

The interior of the trailer was, if anything, even less appealing than its exterior. Kate wouldn't have imagined it possible. The door opened onto a tiny living room, with a threadbare couch running along one wall next to an end table that had been sanded down and never refinished. A wicker chair with a gaping hole in the back sat next to the end table.

A small black and white television was propped atop a dresser on the opposite wall. A frayed electrical cord with no plug attached ran out the back of the set and had been looped over the top. It hung in front of the screen like a broken promise.

A mammoth woman dressed in sweat pants and a stained T-shirt sat at the far end of the couch, legs splayed, eating popcorn out of a bag, shoving handfuls into her mouth. Between bites she slapped playing cards down onto a beat-up coffee table, engrossed in a game of Solitaire.

The woman glanced up disinterestedly at Dani's arrival, and

then returned her attention immediately to her game. She didn't get up to hug her child, who had been gone at least four days, didn't offer her a greeting, didn't acknowledge her presence in any way.

The reason for Dani's attitude was plainly obvious to Kate. The girl was embarrassed. Embarrassed of her home, embarrassed of her mother. Embarrassed of her situation. It would have been difficult enough for an adult to bring someone into this trailer, never mind a thirteen-year-old child.

Dani's mother looked up again. A frown creased her slack features as she noticed Kate for the first time.

"Who're you?" she grunted.

Kate smiled tightly. "A friend of Dani's."

"Yeah? Why're you bringing her home already? She's not due back for another... whatever the hell it is."

Kate felt a flash of annoyance and tamped down on the words that had almost burst out of her mouth of their own accord. She cleared her throat and said, "My name is Kate Messenger."

She crossed the narrow room to the couch and stuck out her hand. The woman stared at it for a moment, then shoved a handful of popcorn into her mouth and wiped her hand on her sweatpants. She gave a perfunctory—and greasy—handshake and said, "I'm Maureen Melanson. Why you bringing the girl home?"

Dani sighed deeply from behind Kate and said, "I'll be in my room."

Kate turned around. "It was wonderful meeting you, Dani," but she was already gone, vanishing down a narrow, dark corridor like a puff of smoke.

Kate returned her attention to the heavyset woman on the couch, who had already grabbed another handful of popcorn.

"Have you seen the news the last few days?"

"News?" the woman said. "Why the hell would I pay attention to the news? You think anything they have to say is gonna affect me here?"

"In this case, yes, that's exactly what I think. If you had watched the news you would have known there was a murder outside the gates of The Mission four nights ago."

The woman stared up at her. "Murder? Is my Billy okay?"

"Yes, none of the children were harmed. It was a counselor who was killed, a young man named Peter LeBlanc."

The almost automatic motion of hand to popcorn bag to mouth had stopped for a moment, but now Maureen Melanson resumed munching her snack with grim relentlessness. She shrugged and spoke while chewing. "What do I care, then? What's it got to do with Dani or Billy?"

Kate couldn't take it anymore. The annoyance she had felt earlier was becoming full-fledged anger, and she said, "What do you care? Really? Are you kidding me? Your son and daughter were present during a murder. Don't you think that might warrant, oh, I don't know, maybe a little of your attention? A little of your precious time? Don't you think maybe you could put down the goddamned cards and get off your goddamned ass and make sure your daughter is okay?"

"I don't appreciate your attitude," Melanson snapped. "I could see the minute the girl came in the door she was fine. There ain't a mark on her."

"Isn't there? Did you see what was on her arm? But forget about that. I'm not talking about her physical health. I'm talking about her mental and emotional well-being. I'm talking about making sure a young child has someone who can comfort her after what has to be one of the most frightening events of her life. I'm talking about paying attention to that girl, not shipping her off to a group home and forgetting about her for a week at a time."

"Yeah? Why don't you get your skinny, meddling ass out of my home and run along and save somebody else. Trust me, Dani was doing fine before you came along and she'll be fine long after you're just a bad memory."

Kate was livid. She couldn't recall the last time she had been this angry. In slightly more than twenty-four hours, she had come to feel extremely protective of Dani.

She didn't trust herself to open her mouth. She wanted to give this woman a piece of her mind as much as she had ever wanted anything in her life, but the trailer was tiny, with paper-thin walls, and she knew with absolute certainty that wherever Dani had gone she was listening to every word. She had already said too much. She wasn't helping Dani's situation and there was nothing she could do *to* help.

She turned on her heel and marched toward the door. Reached out to shove it open and as she did, she caught a glimpse of the girl. Dani had crept back from the hallway and was standing in the shadows of the tiny kitchen in the only place she could be and still remain out of sight of her mother.

"I'm sorry," she whispered, and Kate stopped dead in her tracks. She was surprised to feel tears filling her eyes, and took one step in the girl's direction.

"Oh, honey, you have nothing to be sorry about."

From the couch behind her a shrill voice began screaming, *"Get out of here! Get out! Get the hell out!"*

Kate opened her arms and gave Dani a quick, awkward hug.

Then she slipped out the door, and hurried toward the Rambler.

20

The man with the tattoo sat comfortably on a blanket, his back supported by the trunk of a massive oak tree. He had selected what he felt was the perfect location for his surveillance: far enough into the thickly wooded forest that he would not be easily seen, yet close enough to his target to be afforded a decent view.

Although slightly bored with all the waiting, he couldn't claim to be unhappy, not at the moment. He was still grooving on the high he had gotten from terrorizing the fat bitch from The Mission. He had needed that release, because it had been extremely difficult limiting himself to killing just that weaselly little counselor the other night, especially when so many innocents had been lined up in front of him, ripe and ready for the taking.

In most cases he would have killed every last one of them, kids and adults alike, cutting a swath through that freak house like an avenging angel. He had done exactly that on more than one occasion, and in similar settings as well.

The boy could attest to that.

But this scenario was different, and he was proud of the self-control he had mustered. Because this scenario wasn't about taking as many lives as he could.

This was about sending a message, about making a point.

This was about showing his pursuers exactly who was in charge, about demonstrating in no uncertain terms how unconcerned he was with their feeble pursuit. That he would go wherever he wanted and kill whoever he felt like killing, and there was not a damned thing they could do about it.

And as successful as he had already been in accomplishing his goal, he knew this latest twist in the plan—which he had made up on the fly—would constitute the piece de resistance, the final nail in the coffin of their pathetic, pointless dreams.

A twist as brilliant as it was brutal.

Still, the feeling he had gotten from killing Hamilton and cutting out her tongue was simply sublime. No matter how often he completed his little ritual it never got old, never became stale, never failed to arouse him.

"My lips will not speak wickedness," he mumbled. "Nor my tongue utter deceit."

No tongue could utter deceit when it had been removed from its owner.

But the best part was that he had gotten exactly the information he needed, not that there had been any doubt about that. And once he had the names of the girl's parents, finding their address had taken no more than a couple minutes on the Internet.

The man with the tattoo had visited plenty of remote areas during his time on earth, but few had been more isolated than this —and that was really all he had required.

He had been speedily efficient, too, driving up the interstate to care for his little Lucy—where he kept her at a dump of a motel— before making a one-eighty and returning. He had worked so fast he was able to set up shop out here in the woods of north Lisbon even before the girl's arrival home. So he leaned against the tree and ate his power bars and drank his water, and within twenty minutes the old white station wagon lurched up the dusty driveway and pulled to a stop.

And he was in business.

He watched with interest as Kate Messenger climbed out of the car and escorted Dani Melanson to the trailer. He was close enough that using the binocs wasn't strictly necessary, but he raised them to his face anyway and drank in every exquisite detail of the scene:

The girl's obvious unhappiness at being home.

The strained look on Messenger's face as she walked next to the girl.

It was all very interesting, fascinating even, and he felt his curiosity spike. How in the *hell* had this seemingly normal young girl, in just a couple of days, managed to hook up with the three people who had dedicated their lives to chasing him down?

What was that all about?

It was almost as though their meeting had been preordained by the Devil himself, brought together in their pitiful effort to stop the Lord's work.

"The hand of our God is upon all those for good who seek him, but His power and His wrath are against all those who forsake him."

That was right out of the Bible, and he was about to demonstrate a little wrath of his own.

Fate could be a fickle bitch.

And if it was fate that had brought Dani Melanson into contact with his three hapless friends, it was fate as well that had alerted him to their partnership. That, and a little boy who was so far into his own head he didn't even realize how much he had revealed.

The man with the tattoo kept the glasses glued to the pair as they entered the trailer, the girl first, followed by the ex-cop. For a few minutes nothing happened, and then the sound of a female voice screeching, *"Get out of here! Get out! Get the hell out!"* signaled in no uncertain terms that the brief visit was over.

A couple of seconds later, Messenger burst through the screen door, allowing it to slam closed behind her as she marched resolutely back to the station wagon. The screaming voice chased her to the driveway, and as she slid into the front passenger seat a gaunt-looking older man dressed in dirty jeans and a wife-beater t-shirt opened the trailer's front door.

The man leaned against the doorframe and watched silently as Weston fired up the engine and began backing toward Depot Road. The yelling continued unabated from inside the trailer, and although it didn't seem to bother the hick standing in the doorway, the man with the tattoo felt a spike of annoyance.

The screeching bitch sounded exactly like a cat being disemboweled, and that was from at least fifty feet away. He couldn't imagine how his temper would be affected if he were actually inside the trailer.

No matter. If there was one subject in the world on which he was an expert, it was screaming. His experience with it was life-long, and he had learned years ago that even the most enthusiastic screamer eventually lost interest.

He didn't know what Messenger had said or done during her short stay to set off that fit of caterwauling, but now that she and Weston had departed, the shrew inside that piece of shit tin can should quiet down soon.

He certainly hoped so, anyway, because he intended to wait until nightfall to put his plan into motion. And he didn't want to listen to *that* racket for another three or four hours.

21

"What was that all about?" Weston asked.

He had backed out onto Depot Road and then swung the Rambler back toward Brunswick and hit the gas.

"It should be illegal for some people to procreate," Kate snapped. "That poor girl lost life's lottery in the worst way when she drew that woman for a mother."

Weston looked her over as he drove. "You're really upset," he said, the surprise clear in his tone.

"Damn right I'm upset. That kid deserves better. I'm wondering if we should call social services and report these reprobates."

"And then what? She winds up in the system? What kind of life would that be?"

"Better than the one she's living now."

"You were a cop. You must have seen plenty of situations like hers. Why does this one bother you so much?"

"I don't know," Kate said, and it was true. She had only gone inside to give the mother a heads-up, to let her know she should keep an eye on Dani after what the girl had been through over the last few days. She hadn't intended to get in the woman's face but was unable to stop herself when Melanson exhibited such a lackadaisical attitude toward her child's welfare.

"I have a theory on the subject," Weston said after a moment.

"I'm sure you do. Please, enlighten me."

"You see yourself in that girl."

"That's your brilliant theory? I see myself in her? That's ridiculous. I was nothing like that girl. I didn't grow up in a rusty trailer in the middle of the wilderness. I didn't spend all my free time inside a group home caring for my brother. I didn't—"

"That's not what I mean. I'm talking about personalities. You see a kid whose been forced to grow up fast, and had to deal with things pretty much on her own at a young age. You see a kid who..." His voice trailed off and he shook his head. "You know what? Forget it. It doesn't matter anyway."

She liked you two.

It was the first contribution Chris had made to the conversation other than to complain about returning Dani home, and Kate blinked in surprise.

"Well, I hope she liked us," she said after a moment's hesitation. "We liked her, too."

No, I mean she liked you and Noah taking care of her. She wished we could be her family.

Kate had no response to that. She had no problem ignoring Weston's crackpot theories, but Christopher was another matter entirely. He had claimed once that she possessed powers and abilities similar to his own, but that was a tough pill to swallow, especially after seeing some of the things he could do.

And even if it were true, his abilities were so far advanced over hers—which she considered to be nothing more than a long-time cop's intuition—as to be... well... supernatural.

Which, of course, they were. There could be no other reasonable explanation. So how could she say he didn't know what he was talking about?

"Well, it doesn't really matter," she finally ventured, turning to look at him in the back seat. "Dani has a family of her own and there's nothing we can do to change that. And I'm not gonna apologize for caring about the welfare of that girl."

"Nobody expects you to apologize," Weston said. "It was just an observation, anyway. I wasn't being critical."

He was silent for a moment and then glanced into the rearview mirror at Christopher, who was rocking away in the back seat.

"Are you all right, son? You sound... preoccupied. Like something's bothering you. Something more than bringing Dani home."

I feel him again. He feels close, like maybe he's... I don't know... following us, or watching us. Something. But he's close.

Kate looked over at Weston. His eyes were hooded, his forehead wrinkled in concentration.

"Are you getting anything else?" she asked Chris.

The boy shook his head.

Everything's jumbled. It's too much. It's like a radio with the volume turned up too loud, the sound gets so distorted you can't make anything out.

The boy's words were lost on Kate. She heard them, but any significance they might normally have held was overshadowed by a sudden mix of wonder, confusion, and fear. Because what she saw as she looked at him, simply could not be.

It was impossible.

She forced herself to look away, gazing out the windshield at the thick Maine woods for a full minute as the Rambler crawled along Depot Road. She was overtired, overstressed, that must be it, her exhaustion causing her to see things that weren't there.

She counted to sixty before turning her attention back to Chris, certain that when she did, the thing she thought she had seen before—the impossible thing—would be gone.

Weston was saying something, asking her a question, but his voice was nothing more than a buzzing in the background, like a mosquito flying around at night when she was trying to get to sleep.

Because the thing she had seen was still there.

If anything, it was even a little clearer. Easier to see.

She blinked hard, twice, and looked again.

Still there.

She said, "Chris, did you get bored while I was talking to Dani's mother? Maybe dig up a pen somewhere and draw on yourself?"

What do you mean? he asked, just as Weston said, "What are you talking about?"

She ignored Weston. "So you didn't draw anything on your skin?"

No, Kate. Why would I do that?

She didn't answer.

She *couldn't* answer.

All she could do was stare.

Etched into Christopher's inner wrist, just above his palm and becoming clearer with each passing second, was the symbol with which they had all become intimately familiar.

The symbol that had been tattooed onto the wrist of Peter LeBlanc, Dani Melanson, and every child at the Maine Home for Children with Special Needs four nights ago.

The symbol that Kate Messenger had seen on the wrist of her mother's killer through the killer's own eyes.

The circumpunct.

A circle with a dot in the middle.

22

Nightfall seemed to take forever to come. Under the thick forest canopy, dusk settled in early but lingered impossibly long.

And with the failing light came hordes of mosquitoes. They swarmed around the man with the tattoo, attacking every square inch of exposed flesh. After a few minutes spent trying to tough it out he began slapping at them, waving his hands in a futile attempt to shoo them away, counting on the denseness of the trees and underbrush to keep him hidden from sight of anyone who might glance out one of the trailer's windows and spot the movement.

Normally, anticipation was the sweetest fruit imaginable. He enjoyed teasing himself, putting off the nearly orgasmic release of the hunt until he simply couldn't stand waiting anymore. And then he would wait just a little longer.

But tonight, with these damned mosquitoes, the sweet anticipation never truly materialized. The distraction was too great. He was itchy and annoyed and anxious. Short-tempered.

Still, he waited. He was too thorough, too meticulous, too good at what he did to deviate from a well thought-out plan simply because of something as minor as a few flesh-eating insects. Or even more than a few. They could chew on him all night if they wanted, they could drink a pint of his blood, and it wouldn't matter. He would not allow himself to be rushed.

He would stick with his plan, which was to wait until full dark, and then approach the trailer as stealthily as possible. Because he had seen homes like this rust-bucket trailer before, had known a few people who owned places exactly like it. Had even visited one not that long ago in the little dirtwater town of Singer, Alabama.

And in every single case, the resident had been armed to the teeth.

He supposed it was possible *this* homeowner might not own a thirty-ought rifle or a goddamned Desert Eagle .50 cal that could blow his head practically off his shoulders, but he wasn't prepared to bet his life on it.

So he would wait as long as necessary, approach under cover of darkness, and then bust through the weak-ass piece of aluminum and screen mesh masquerading as a front door with no warning. He would swarm all over the family like ants on a picnic lunch, and it wouldn't matter how many weapons the man of the house might own, they would be useless because he would never be able to get his hands on them in time to do him any good.

That was the plan and it was a good one, so the fucking mosquitoes could kiss his ass. They weren't the only ones with a taste for blood, and he would do whatever it took, wait however *long* it took, to enjoy that taste.

There had been not a single sign of life in the trailer since the screaming stopped shortly after Kate Messenger and her two friends left.

That was hours ago. No one had come or gone. Lights had come on inside the trailer, weak and flickering, but not a sound had drifted out of the rusty tin can. No television, no radio, no talking or laughing.

Nothing.

But the man with the tattoo knew the family was still inside. They had to be, because the first thing he had done when he arrived was to ensure there wasn't a second doorway that might allow his quarry to slip away unnoticed while he was sitting on his ass watching the front of the trailer.

And there wasn't any second door. No windows big enough for anyone to crawl through. Nothing.

So no matter how quiet it might be, the family was still in there.

Ripe for the taking.

He looked straight up, straining to catch a glimpse of light, but there was nothing. It was virtually impossible to differentiate the tops of the trees from the inky nighttime sky.

Finally, full darkness had fallen.
It was time to go to work.

23

The minute they had closed and locked the motel room door, Kate and Weston began an up-close examination of the mark on Christopher's wrist. They traced it with their fingers, their concern palpable. Kate bounced back and forth between disbelief and fear.

It looked exactly like a tattoo, but one that had been embedded under the skin for decades, with none of the tender redness Kate had seen on Dani, or the children at The Mission.

"This can't be possible," she said, looking pointedly at Christopher. "Are you sure you didn't draw this?"

I'm sure, Kate. Why would I lie?

He had been known to withhold information in the past, but he was right. There was no reason for him to lie.

Weston had tried scrubbing it with a washcloth, using soap and warm water, but hadn't been able to smudge it, let alone wash it away.

Like a tattoo.

There was no explanation. Its origin was a mystery—another one—and would remain so, at least for the time being.

Could it have something to do with their close proximity to the Beast? Could this somehow be related to his little exercise in mind control?

He had managed to prevent them from remembering what he looked or sounded like—so, was this his way of taunting them? Of making sure they knew exactly why they'd felt so uncomfortable in the presence of Detective Bannerman?

Maybe the circumpunct would disappear as mysteriously as it had appeared. Maybe its stain would remain on Christopher for the rest of his life, a permanent and unwelcome obscenity.

Maybe, God forbid, this was only the beginning, and identical markings would start to appear on other parts of his body.

Maybe they would appear on Weston and Kate as well.

There was no way to tell. All they could do at this point was wait and see. But Kate would be lying to herself if she didn't admit she was spooked. The symbol had to be related to the Beast, there was no other reasonable explanation. And until she uncovered how they were linked, she knew the sick feeling would remain in the pit of her stomach.

All the more reason to track down the Beast and end this nightmare once and for all, to turn over every rock between Maine and California, if that was what it took, until Bonner or Beaumont or Bannerman—or whatever he was calling himself these days—slithered out from under one like the poisonous snake he was.

And then eliminate him.

The old Kate Messenger would never have considered killing another human being, no matter how slimy and repugnant, other than in self-defense—or under extenuating circumstances.

Arrest and prosecution, sure. Every day of the week and twice on Sunday.

But not flat-out murder.

But this mysterious marking on Christopher's arm was just the latest horror in a seemingly unending series of horrors to befall them. It didn't help that they now knew that the Beast was what Weston had so aptly called a phantom. His ability to "disguise" himself, to cloud their memory, meant they'd have to be more vigilant than ever.

Kate still believed in her heart their first option should be to try to take him into custody—assuming that was even possible. But after all she had seen and experienced over the last few months, any lingering reservations she had about snuffing him out now took a back seat to ridding the world of the scourge that was the Beast.

Besides, the more she saw of his handiwork, the more she observed of the depravity he was capable of inflicting on society's most helpless and innocent victims, the less she thought of him as human.

He was subhuman.

A monster.

And he deserved to die.

Kate realized her hands had begun to shake. She was breathing heavily, almost panting. Weston was staring at her in concern and she hated that. She had to take a step back and get a grip on her emotions.

Christopher's blank eyes were trained on her, and despite his blindness, he had the uncanny ability to read her.

It's okay, Kate. I'm fine. I can't even feel it.

This from the kid who had actually suffered the attack on his body. He was a child and he was handling this latest assault better than the adult, better than the woman who was supposed to be the no-nonsense professional.

He said, *We'll get through this. I don't know why this thing showed up on my wrist, but we'll figure it out and we'll deal with it, just like we've dealt with everything else.*

Kate breathed deeply and forced a smile onto her face. Even though Christopher couldn't see it, she hoped he'd at least feel it..

"I know we will," she said.

She glanced at Weston and noted the relief in his expression, the thankfulness that she had pulled herself together. The caring. And she hated that almost as much as she had hated his pitying gaze a few seconds ago.

"Anyway," she continued, thankful her voice remained more or less steady. "It's obvious we're not going to figure this out right now, so I suppose we should move on to something we *can* control: where we go from here."

"And where's that?" Weston asked.

"Back to The Mission. Give Chris a chance to spend more time there. Do a proper gathering. After everything that's happened in that place—especially after this morning—he should find plenty to draw from." She looked at Chris. "Assuming you're up for that."

I was thinking the same thing. I'm sorry I let you down today.

"We've been over this. You don't need to apologize."

"There's just one problem," Weston said. "How do we get

access? Hamilton made it clear she never wants to see us again."

"Do you really give a damn what she wants?"

"Not really, no."

"Neither do I," Kate said. "But I don't want to just show up there unannounced again. Especially at night. Those poor kids have been through enough already. And if we go there and try to storm the gates, the staff will call the cops and have us dragged right out of there."

Weston shrugged. "Maybe we don't have to storm the gates. Maybe Chris can get what we need from outside the building."

The boy shook his head. *I already tried. I need to be closer to where it all happened.*

"Okay," Weston said. "So, it's inside or nothing." He looked at Kate. "And I know you don't want to disturb those kids, but we should probably talk to some of them. Just because Dani couldn't tell us anything, doesn't mean the same is true for anyone else. He inked them all. And if we're lucky, he didn't consider them a threat, so he may not have felt the need to play hide and seek with their short term memories."

"Maybe not," Kate said. "But they could still be tough to get through to. Especially if they're frightened."

"We have to try. Make it like a game or something, while Chris does his thing. But in order to do that, we'll need the staff's cooperation. Which brings us back to Hamil..." Weston stopped, looking as if he'd swallowed something poisonous.

"What is it?" Kate asked. "What's wrong?"

"Bannerman. The Beast."

"What about him?"

"I've been trying to remember what he said to us today, but it's all jumbled in my brain."

"Right," Kate said. "It's the same for me."

"But just now something poked through, something about Hamilton. Did he tell her he was coming back? For further questioning?"

Kate thought about it and drew a blank. "I don't know. I don't remember. But why would he? He wasn't there for her. He was there to taunt us."

"Maybe so, but if she's in any danger, that's all the more reason to call her. I don't particularly care for the woman, but if that son of the bitch went after her..."

Kate nodded, grabbed her purse, then found her phone and dialed, waiting as the line buzzed in her ear.

After a half-dozen rings the call was connected and a recorded voice said, "This is the Maine Home for Children with Special Needs. Our offices are currently closed, but if you leave your name, number and a brief message, we'll get back to you as soon as we can. If this is an emergency, please press one now to connect to one of our—"

Kate pressed the number and the line rang again. After a moment, a woman answered. "Maine Home for Children with Special Needs. This is Livvie Barnstead. How may I help you?"

"*Livvie*? You're still there?"

"Who *is* this?"

"Kate Karlson. The woman who—"

"I remember. What the hell do you want?"

The fear Barnstead had exhibited that morning had completely vanished. Now she simply sounded surly.

"Why are you there so late?" Kate asked.

"I work a split shift, if it's any of your business. What's this about?"

"Jane Hamilton. Did someone come to visit her after we left? A detective named Bannerman?"

"No, nobody showed up, and it wouldn't have mattered if they did. She went home just a few minutes after you three left. Said she wasn't feeling well."

No big surprise there. "So you think she's at home now?"

"What do I know? I'm not her keeper. Look, why can't you people just leave us alone? We did what we were supposed to do, so go to hell and don't bother us again."

The line clicked in Kate's ear before she had a chance to respond.

She sighed. "That didn't go so well."

"Yeah, I kinda got that impression. Call her back and get Hamilton's home number."

"Not gonna happen," Kate said. "Barnstead would just as soon we dropped off the face of the earth. But I don't think there's anything to worry about. She said Bannerman didn't show."

"Why doesn't that make me feel any better?"

Kate shrugged. "There's not much we can do about it. I can run a check, but Hamilton doesn't strike me as the type to make her home address and phone number easily accessible, so we might have to wait until morning and try her office again."

Weston frowned. "I hate waiting. Especially when we're so close. And I can't help feeling things are slipping out of control."

I can't help feeling we've never been in control.

Kate and Weston shared a troubled glance. She wanted to disagree, to reassure Christopher, but couldn't think of a single thing to say.

24

Things got strange after Christopher fell asleep.

Assuming the word *strange* had any meaning at this point.

He was sprawled across one of the beds as the rerun of an ancient sitcom flickered on the motel television, the sound turned low.

Weston sat in a shabby armchair, only half-watching the show as Kate sat on the second bed, fingers flying over her laptop keyboard.

The name Hamilton was even more common in this area than the name Melanson, and a search for the woman's home address and phone number had yielded six "Janes," twenty listed merely as "J," a "J.E.," a "J.T." and a "J.W."

Kate supposed she could call them all, but there was no guarantee that any of them were the person she sought, and intuition told her she'd be wasting her time. In the unlikely event that the Beast actually *had* gone after Hamilton, Kate highly doubted the woman would still be alive.

She hated to sound so cavalier about that possibility, but months of hunting this psychopath had hardened her to the realities of her new life.

So she had decided to switch gears entirely. Do a different kind of search, digging into historical databases and newspaper archives. And when an article filled her screen, she froze, not quite believing what she'd found.

She felt Weston observing her out of the corner of his eye and knew he must have heard her catch her breath.

"You okay over there?"

No, she was definitely not okay. Not by a long shot. Not if what she was staring at had any basis in reality.

"Kate?"

She kept her gaze on the computer screen. "Nothing," she said. "It's nothing. This has to be some kind of Internet glitch. Either that, or I may need to check myself into a psych ward."

"What are you talking about? Is this about Hamilton?"

"No, I've moved on from her. We'll just have to try her tomorrow."

"Then what's got you so spooked?"

She tore her gaze from the screen and looked up at him. "This is the second time that we know of that the Beast has targeted a group home."

"And?"

"I figured that couldn't be a coincidence. That there has to be some significance to it. The group home setting means something to him."

Weston nodded. "That makes sense. Except in the attack against Chris's home, he killed everyone in sight. This time, he only killed one. The situations are very different."

She waved her hand. "They're only different because he wanted to make a point. And his point was made more dramatic by the fact that he allowed the children to live."

"And that point is?"

"He's obviously trying to tell us that we're puppets on his string, and if we refuse to dance to his tune, next time he *will* kill everyone. So the situations are different but the same, if you see what I'm saying."

Weston considered her logic for a moment. "Okay. But that still doesn't explain why you look like you've just witnessed a botched execution."

"I was thinking, what if this is part of a pattern we haven't considered. What if this *isn't* just the second time he's attacked a group home."

"Right," Weston said. "I get that. So you're searching for similar crimes, and I'm guessing you found something significant."

"Yes," she said. "But that's where things get strange."

"In what way?"

She glanced down at her laptop's screen, then looked back up at Weston and shook her head. "This is too crazy to make any sense."

"*What's* too crazy? Jesus Christ, Kate, just tell me what you found."

"All right, listen to this." She looked down at her computer and read, "United Press International. Out of Tallahassee. 'A bloody rampage through a group home overnight left nine people—seven of them children—dead in a murder spree that has stunned authorities for its unprecedented brutali—'"

"Wait a minute, hold on," Weston said. "Tallahassee? That's not separate or different. That's the home where Chris was living. And after the attack he bounced around in the system for awhile before moving in with the Haneys."

"You asked what's spooking me. Can I finish?"

"Fine," he said, "but we know all this already."

Kate sucked in a breath, then continued reading. "There is also some confusion about the death toll. Initially, police said they discovered ten bodies in the home. A source at the coroner's office, however, said nine bodies arrived at the morgue." She looked up at him. "There's more, but you get the idea."

"I don't have to 'get the idea,'" Weston said. "None of this is new information. The reason for the discrepancy in body count was because Christopher died and came back. He told you that."

She stared at him without speaking. Opened her mouth and closed it.

"You're scaring me, Kate. I'm starting to wonder if you're right about that psych ward. What the hell is wrong with you?"

"What's wrong with me is the date," she said.

"What are you talking about? What date?"

She pointed at the screen. "The date of this news report."

Weston spread his hands and grunted in exasperation. "What about it? Chris was seven at the time of the attack, and if I remember correctly, it happened near the beginning of—."

"May 4th," Kate said. "That's what he told me. So this article should be dated May 5th, 2011. When Chris was seven years old."

Weston was at a loss. "So I assume it isn't? Is that your earth-shattering news? Did they somehow miss their deadline and print it on the sixth instead?"

She shook her head. "Come over here and see for yourself."

Weston scowled, pushed himself out of the chair, then moved to the bed and sat next to her.

She angled the laptop so he could see the screen. Watched as he scanned the report, mumbling to himself. "Shane Cornell, United Press Inter..."

His voice trailed off and he sat openmouthed, staring at the screen in disbelief.

"Now you know what's got me so spooked," she said.

The article describing the carnage at Christopher's group home was indeed dated May 5th.

May 5th, *1995.*

25

Overcast skies blotted out the moon and stars as the man with the tattoo moved slowly, stealthily, quietly toward the rusted house trailer.

His heart was racing and he found he was breathing heavily, not from fear but from anticipation. He was hunting, and hunting was his favorite pastime in the world. Hunting was better than the satisfying ending of a good book, better than the dessert after a good meal, better than the climax after great sex.

Hunting *was* great sex.

In fact, it was everything. It made life worth living. Maybe not for the hunted, but definitely for the hunter.

He took his time, enjoying his heightened senses and the feeling of the blood pumping through his veins. He kept his eyes moving in a continuous scan, his gaze flicking from the trailer to the driveway to the ground in front of him, cognizant of the possibility of tripping over a fallen log or stepping on a small dead branch and snapping it, giving away his presence.

Realistically, the odds of *seeing* any branches before stepping on them in this darkness were slim, but there was value in being thorough, and no downside to sweeping the ground with his eyes before each step. His prey wasn't going anywhere, and whether it took two minutes to get to the house or twenty was irrelevant.

The lights had gone off inside the trailer more than an hour ago, and the home was still and quiet. He would have bet his last buck that the family was fast asleep by now.

His reward for the judicious exercise of patience.

The sounds of the dark forest resonated around him. From somewhere to the north an owl hooted, the sound mournful and lonely. A dog—or maybe a coyote—howled at the nighttime sky. Off in the distance a loon sounded its eerie cry. Small animals crept through the brush even as he did the same.

He thought of them hunting, as he was doing, and smiled.

He wasn't afraid. Wasn't nervous. He was in his element, a predator stalking its prey.

He reached the edge of the clearing surrounding the dilapidated trailer and paused. Took one last long look at his surroundings, turning three hundred sixty degrees, convincing himself he was truly alone. Then he set off across the clearing, moving without hesitation toward the screen door.

When he reached it, he didn't pause.

He barely slowed.

He climbed the small wooden landing and flicked open his box cutter. Sliced out a six-inch semicircle of screen and undid the latch. Couldn't believe how stupid these hicks were, making it so easy for someone like him to get inside.

He pulled the screen door open, moving slowly to minimize the warning screech the ancient hinges tried to emit.

But then he could have hired a marching band to play John Philip Sousa's "Stars and Stripes Forever" as he entered the home and it wouldn't have made a damn bit of difference.

The man of the house could have a semi-auto pistol under his pillow and it wouldn't matter now.

Because the Beast was hunting, and when he was hunting he was invincible. He was a lion inside the lamb's den, relentless and all-powerful, and now that he was here, the end result was inevitable.

He would not stop until he had taken what he came for and the hunt was finished.

26

The silence in the motel room stretched on until Kate thought it might last forever.

The only sound was Christopher snoring softly nearby. It was often impossible to tell whether the boy was asleep or awake, but there was no doubt at the moment.

He had asked to sleep in here again tonight rather than go into Weston's room. Maybe because he missed Dani, and this was where they'd first cuddled up.

Weston himself had stayed as well, slumped quietly in the armchair, staring at the wall, unable or unwilling to force himself to get up and go to bed.

The time was now after midnight, but there was no way Kate could fall asleep. She wasn't sure she would ever sleep again.

The newspaper article she had unearthed online had left her with a sense of deep-seated unease, a feeling that couldn't have been worse if the Beast himself were occupying the room with them.

And in a sense he was, because the corruption of his presence filled Kate's brain, her soul, and one look at Weston told her he felt the same.

Earlier, Kate had moved off the bed and taken a seat at the small writing desk near Weston's chair, in an attempt to avoid waking Christopher while they discussed the significance of the news article, which was clearly impossible but just as clearly real.

Detail for detail, it was identical to everything Kate had learned about the attack that had left everyone in Chris's group home dead, including Chris for a time. But obviously even the youngest of children who had survived an attack in 1995 would be in his or her twenties today, and for all of Christopher's uniqueness, an inability to age didn't seem to be included in his bag of tricks.

After a long silence, Weston cleared his throat. Started to speak and then stopped.

Started again and stopped.

"What is it?" Kate prompted. "This isn't the time to be bashful. If you have something to say, let's talk about it."

"Okay," he said, then paused again, as if weighing his words. "What if the Beast placed that article online himself? You know, wrote it up and somehow managed to archive it among other UPI stories from that year?"

Kate shook her head. "For what purpose? I mean, I suppose it's technically possible he could have fabricated the whole thing, including quotes from police reps and witnesses, but what would be the point? What guarantee would there even be that we would see it?"

Weston considered the question for a moment. "It would be reasonable for him to assume that after his attack on The Mission we might research similar attacks. He would expect us to make the connection, don't you think?"

"Probably. But the notion of him expending the effort to fake a twenty year old news article and then bury it online where there was no guarantee it would ever be seen by *anyone*, let alone us, seems like a stretch. Even for a guy who likes to play games." She sighed. "If anything, it tells me we might be getting a little paranoid."

Weston pursed his lips. "Paranoid? Kate, everything that has happened in this city has been directed at us. Murdering LeBlanc and cutting out his tongue was done specifically to get enough media attention to ensure we would see it. Tattooing those children and then forcing Livvie Barnstead to memorize his message was done because he knew we would come running. It was all orchestrated for our benefit, so don't tell me I'm being paranoid."

"Okay, maybe 'paranoid' was the wrong word to use. But I'm still not convinced that planting some obscure news article is this guy's style."

Weston gazed at her without speaking.

"Think about it," she pressed. "You of all people understand his methods. He's straightforward and brutal, a monster to whom subtlety is as foreign a concept as empathy or mercy."

Weston remained silent and she said, "Murdering Peter LeBlanc and removing his tongue fits his personality. Tattooing innocent children fits his personality. Crafting a fake news story and burying it online?" She shook her head.

"I don't disagree with you, Kate, but just because he's capable of such awful brutality doesn't automatically mean he's *not* capable of subtlety as well, when the mood suits him. When it comes down to it, we really know nothing about this guy. We know only what he's revealed through his twisted actions. We already learned something new about him this morning. What he's capable of. And there may well be much more we have yet to learn. I don't think we can rule anything out at this point."

It was Kate's turn to be silent, and after a moment Weston continued. "I think there's every possibility he's equally capable of brutality *and* subtlety, mixed together into one rotting psychopathic stew."

Kate sat back, considering his point. He was right. There was plenty they didn't know about the Beast. But the idea that he could have faked and planted a UPI story from 1995 on the off chance that they'd stumble across it, was not only laughable, but a kind of creative deception that would indicate a level of psychological cunning that made Hannibal Lecter seem like Mother Teresa of Calcutta.

"I just don't buy it," she said, shaking her head. "What motive would he have? What does he accomplish by making us believe the attack on Chris happened twenty years ago instead of four?"

"To do exactly what it's done," Noah said. "To screw with our heads. Throw us off our game." He nodded toward Christopher. "To make us wonder about who—or what—it is we're traveling with."

"Sorry, Noah. For me, that's a bridge too far."

"So then what's the alternative? A glitch on the website?"

"That was my first inclination," she said, then gestured to the computer screen. "But look at it. It's not a blog entry. It's an actual scanned copy of the print version of the paper. Part of their digital archives."

"So are you saying you think it's real?"

They stared at each other. The shadows cast by the weak motel lighting washed out half of Weston's face, rendering it fuzzy and indistinct. He looked tired, haunted, like a man who was losing himself.

She supposed that was an apt description.

She sighed. "I don't know what I'm saying. But there's no way to explain away two separate attacks, over fifteen years apart, that are identical to each other in every conceivable way, including a missing dead person."

They glanced at Christopher. Still snoring.

Weston pushed out a breath. "Should we wake him up? Ask him straight out if we've lost our minds?"

"I'm not sure I want to hear his answer."

"Neither am I. So maybe we should get some sleep. Clear our heads and figure this out tomorrow."

"I don't think that's possible right now."

Weston nodded. "You're right. I'm wide awake. Especially now."

A tortured moan sounded rose from the other bed. Kate looked over to see Christopher tossing and turning. He appeared to still be asleep, but was obviously agitated.

"Nightmare?" she said, moving toward the boy.

She had gotten to know Chris pretty well over the last several months, but still felt less than comfortable dealing with an eleven-year-old. When it came to caregiving, her preference was to defer to the man who had been watching over him for much longer.

"Looks like it," Weston said. "I'm surprised he doesn't have more of them."

"No kidding."

As she got close to the bed, she saw that Chris's face was red and he seemed to be sweating. He rolled over, turning his back to her, and then flipped positions again a moment later. He was gasping now, high-pitched cries of panic that echoed off the stark walls and around the room.

"Ah, ah, ah." The sound was heartbreaking.

His legs kicked as if he was running in his dream, and Kate turned toward Weston.

"Something's wrong," she said, and Weston clearly agreed. He had risen to a half-standing position and his eyes were fixed on the boy. He stepped forward now, moving hesitantly toward the bed.

Kate's concern was edging closer to panic. "We'd better wake him."

"Probably a good idea," Weston said, and took another couple of steps in the boy's direction.

And then Christopher woke up, bursting out of sleep with a strangled cry like a drowning swimmer breaking the surface of a lake.

"Ah, ah, ah," he said, because that was all he *could* say as he rolled off the bed and landed on his feet. His head swiveled wildly, and he stared blankly in their direction as the desperate cries continued, and then he turned toward the tiny bathroom.

Looking rail thin and small, he sprinted through the doorway and slammed the door behind him. A half-second later Kate heard the toilet seat clank against the water tank with a half-metallic, half-plastic *crack*. And then Chris puked, the contents of his stomach splattering wetly into the bowl as he gasped and continued the awful "ah, ah, ah" cries between rounds of vomiting.

Weston burst through the door, Kate right behind him. Christopher was sitting on the floor, leaning back against the wall next to the sink. A thin sheen of sweat covered his crimson face and he panted as he tried to catch his breath.

Weston crouched next to him. "What's wrong? Are you sick? Is it something you ate?"

He placed the back of his hand against Christopher's forehead, checking for a fever, but Chris shook his head weakly.

I'm not sick. At least, not with a fever.

"Then what's the matter?" Weston asked.

It's Dani.

Weston and Kate shared a look of surprise and Kate crouched down beside them.

"What about her?" she said.

I...I don't know. Something's wrong.

"What do you mean? What's wrong with her?"

I'm not sure. I can't tell. But it's bad. It's really bad. We have to get to her house right now.

Kate glanced at her watch. "Christopher, it's after midnight. We can't go out there now. After what happened this afternoon, I don't think we can—"

You don't understand. Something's wrong, something's really wrong, she's in trouble and we have to go now. Not tomorrow, not later. Now. We have to leave right now.

Kate immediately got to her feet. She had seen Chris like this before and knew that he would continue to insist until they did as he asked. He was like a dog with a bone when he got this way and he would not give up until they were on the road and headed to Dani's place.

That wasn't what bothered her.

What bothered her was his tone. He sounded desperate and afraid, in a way she had never heard him before.

Weston stared at Chris for a moment, then looked up and said, "I don't think we have a choice. Let's get dressed and go."

27

If Depot Road had seemed remote during the day—and it had—the narrow, pothole-strew pavement was positively alien at night. Streetlights were nonexistent, and with a storm seemingly imminent, the darkness surrounding the Rambler's overmatched headlights was as impenetrable as anything Kate had ever seen.

Weston drove in silence. Christopher had calmed somewhat, but every so often he moaned softly in the back seat, the only indication he hadn't fallen back to sleep. Given his barely restrained panic back at the motel, Kate doubted he was even capable of sleeping.

The going was slow, even slower than it had been this afternoon—*yesterday* afternoon, Kate reminded herself, since it was now nearly one a.m.

Something's very wrong, Chris said. *Can't we go any faster?*

"What are you feeling?" Kate asked.

Nothing.

"What do you mean? How do you know something's wrong if you're not feeling or hearing anything?"

That's exactly how I know. Back at the motel, I could sense Dani's pain, her terror. It woke me up it was so real. It was as clear as anything I've ever felt.

"But now it's gone."

Yes. Now there's nothing. Just like with Lucy. When I lost contact with her.

Kate knew his heart must be breaking.

"Maybe that's a good sign," she said hopefully. "Maybe that means that whatever was bothering her is over. Maybe it means she's sleeping quietly now."

144

Maybe, he agreed, but it was obvious he didn't believe it.

Can't we go any faster? he said again.

Weston glanced at him in the rearview mirror. "This road is nasty, Chris, but it won't be long now. We're almost there."

And they were. Kate recognized the sharp turn in the road far in the distance, a nearly ninety-degree angle to the right barely visible in the outer reaches of the headlights. She recalled thinking how dangerous it was to engineer a road with that kind of a turn for drivers to navigate. She remembered also that the Melansons' driveway was only another hundred or so yards beyond that turn.

Massive evergreens, ancient maples, and oaks crowded in on the Rambler. Ghostly white birches slid past on either side, clustered together, huddled against an oncoming storm, their spindly branches reaching out to clutch at the car like spectral arms and fingers.

Kate shivered, suddenly certain that if those arms and fingers should get a grip on the car, they would pull it off the road and drag it into the forest where it would be lost in the thick underbrush. They would never be seen again.

"Jesus," she muttered.

"What is it?" Weston asked.

"Nothing. I just need to get it together."

"It's been a long few days."

"It's been a long few months. *More* than a few."

"No argument there."

"Pull over," she said suddenly.

"Why?"

"Because we're almost there."

"So?"

"Just pull over and kill the headlights. Do it now."

Weston shot her a glance, then eased the car to the side of the road. It didn't take much; the side and the middle of Depot Road were practically the same thing. He punched a knob on the dash and the lights disappeared, plunging the car and its occupants into total darkness.

Kate reached forward until her knuckles banged against the

dash. She scrabbled for the glove box release. Pulled at it and missed. Said with exasperation, "Turn on the interior light."

Weston complied and Kate opened the glove box. She reached inside and wrapped her fingers around her Beretta. It felt solid and reassuring in her hand, which she realized without much surprise was shaking slightly as adrenaline flooded her system. Then she reached into her purse and grasped a full magazine. It was placed atop a pair of surgical gloves, and she removed those as well, slipping them into the front pocket of her jeans. Finally, she pulled her Mag light and a San Diego Padres baseball cap out from under her seat. She jammed the hat on her head.

Weston had watched her without speaking to this point. Now he said, "I'm not positive, Kate, but I don't think the State of Maine recognizes your Texas carry permit."

She checked the mag quickly and then slammed it home and chambered a round. Then she looked up at Weston. "I don't think I care."

"Okay," he said slowly. "What now?"

"Now you turn the interior lights back off."

"You know what I mean," he said, turning the knob.

"The plan is simple. You two sit here while I go see if anything is happening inside that trailer."

"I'm going with you."

"No, you're not."

"Are you out of your mind? You can't go marching up there by yourself."

Kate turned to Weston. "We don't have time to argue about this. We're not bringing Chris into a situation that's a total question mark, and leaving him alone isn't an option either."

"It wouldn't be the first time."

"And that excuses it? No, you both stay put until I get a handle on what's going on."

Please go. Please hurry. Something's wrong, something—

"I know," she said. "I'm going right now."

She turned to Weston again. "I hate leaving you here with no way to defend yourself. Maybe I should leave the Beretta with you."

"Forget it," he said.

"Noah, I know how you feel about—"

"Yes, you do, and I said forget it. It's bad enough you're leaving me here to twiddle my thumbs while you go into god knows what. We're sitting in an idling car, surrounded by two tons of Detroit steel. If I see anything threatening I'll hit the horn to warn you, then drive away and come back for you later. Don't worry about Chris and me. We'll be fine."

Kate, please. Go.

She reached for the door handle. "Once I know everything's secure up there I'll be back. It shouldn't take long."

"This is a bad idea," Weston said.

"If you have a better one, I'm all ears."

The silence formed his answer.

Kate! Please!

She opened the door and stepped into the darkness of the Maine night.

28

Walking Depot Road was even more difficult than driving it had been. Kate didn't feel comfortable using her flashlight until she knew what she was getting into, so she stumbled along the sandy verge in the dark, expecting at any moment to step into a pothole and break her ankle.

After what felt like half an hour but was probably only two or three minutes she arrived at the ridiculous ninety-degree turn in the road. This meant the Melansons' trailer was getting close, making stealth now her number one priority. She was entering an uncertain situation, armed with a single semi-automatic pistol and no backup.

It was not ideal.

She tried to calm her jittery nerves by telling herself she might not be walking into anything dangerous at all. Maybe Christopher had simply suffered through a frighteningly realistic nightmare, and she would arrive at the trailer to find nothing more sinister than a sleeping family, two parents frightened and more than a little angry at being awakened in the middle of the night by the last person in the world they expected—or wanted—to see.

But as much as she tried to convince herself of this scenario, she couldn't quite pull it off. She had been with Christopher plenty long enough by now to know exactly what he was capable of, and if he said Dani was in trouble, then there was a damned good chance something was wrong.

She just wished his vision, or his intuition, or whatever the hell it was, had been a little more specific.

The road seemed to narrow further as she walked. Tree branches rendered invisible by the near-total darkness scraped her arms and legs and even the side of her face as she passed.

I hate Maine, she thought randomly. Vacationland, my ass. Give me sunny southern California any day.

The Melansons' driveway was upon her almost before she realized it. She had been thinking about home, daydreaming, and damned near walked right past the place. She shook her head, angry with herself. Inattention to the task at hand could get her killed faster than anything else, especially in this type of situation.

She stopped in her tracks. Mentally refocused. Developed the bare-bones outline of a plan. She would take her time and circle the trailer in the dark, examine it from all angles and look for anything that seemed out of place. If all appeared normal, then she would have no choice but to climb the front landing and pound on that flimsy screen door until rousing someone out of bed. Then she would explain... what? That a pre-teen psychic had warned her through mental telepathy that something was wrong out here, so she had jumped in her car and sped out to investigate?

Dani's parents would think she was insane, and Kate wouldn't blame them. Hopefully she could avoid getting shot if nothing else.

None of these misgivings mattered. Either she trusted Christopher's instincts or she didn't.

No matter who or what he really was.

She thought about the UPI article and what its implications might be. Two identical crimes occurring more than fifteen years apart. She thought about Chris's confession to her all those months ago—that he had died the night he was attacked, only to be revived.

He was clearly alive now. She had held him and cared for him and shared meals with him and laughed with him.

But the date of that article weighed on her, *frightened* her, and she shuddered at the thought that the Christopher she knew might not be what he seemed to be. If the Beast could alter people's ability to see him as he really was, did that mean Chris was capable of it as well? Was he merely presenting himself to them as a young blind boy in order to garner their sympathy?

She pushed the thought away. It was too ridiculous to waste time on.

Maybe Weston had been right. Maybe that article was the Beast's handiwork, doing his best to fuck with their minds.

And she'd be damned if she'd give him that pleasure.

She began moving once again, advancing slowly up the rutted driveway. A weak yellow glow came into view from inside the trailer, barely strong enough to penetrate the gauzy curtain hanging over the small kitchen window.

She melted into the tree line as she approached the home, uneasy but uncertain exactly why.

The trailer was still. Silent. If anyone was awake inside, that person wasn't moving around.

Kate turned her attention away from the window and as she did, a stiff breeze gusted through the clearing, causing the tops of the ancient trees to rustle and moan.

A weak scream sounded from the vicinity of the trailer and then was cut off.

Kate froze, focusing on the front of the trailer, cursing the darkness, gripping her Beretta a little more firmly.

She heard the sound again and once again it disappeared, and she realized she wasn't hearing a scream at all. It was nothing more than the annoying screech of the rusty hinges she had heard yesterday afternoon as she pulled open the trailer's aluminum screen door.

But the realization did little to quell her rising concern. If the door was screeching in the breeze, then it obviously was not latched. She tried to recall whether there had been a problem with the latch when she entered and departed the trailer and didn't think so.

Someone had not bothered to close the door properly. Given the amount of noise it was making—and the screeching sound was becoming more insistent as the breeze picked up—it seemed inconceivable that no one would be getting up to close it. Even the laziest of homeowners or the deepest of sleepers would have trouble ignoring that racket.

Someone should be getting out of bed and stumbling to the

damned door to latch it.

But nobody was.

It was time to modify the plan. If she had wanted an indication whether there really was a problem in the Melanson home, the noisy screen door provided it. Even without Christopher's intuition, the sound of that door swinging and banging in the wind would have been enough to convince her cop brain that something was wrong.

She reached into her pocket, pulled out the gloves, and snapped them on, thankful she had decided to bring them along. It was starting to look more and more that leaving fingerprints—or any evidence of her presence—might be a mistake.

She tried to recall if she'd left any prints during her earlier visit, but could only remember hugging Dani and touching that door.

She struggled through the underbrush, moving along the side of the trailer with greater urgency. She walked just far enough past the corner to get a glimpse behind the house, wanting the reassurance that no one was lurking back there, ready to ambush her when she stepped out of the woods.

But that reassurance would not come easy.

It would not come at all.

She simply couldn't see enough to satisfy herself. If someone was behind the house, that person was either well hidden or simply invisible in the darkness. Kate could see no movement beyond the mangled chain hanging from the swing set, which creaked back and forth in the freshening wind.

She retraced her steps until reaching a point roughly parallel to the trailer's front wall. Slipped her flashlight into the waistband of her jeans. Then she broke cover, crossing the weedy yard at a trot, gun held at her side in both hands.

When she reached the trailer, she flattened herself against the wall and began edging toward the door. The wind was picking up quickly, whipping stray strands of hair that had escaped her cap around her face, as the door slammed against the aluminum siding in a frenzied screech-bang, screech-bang, screech-bang.

The sound was louder here, more insistent. Kate moved slowly along the wall until she reached the landing, and then bounded up the stairs as quietly as she could. The wind and the racket provided more than adequate cover for any noise she might be making, but the noise was a double-edged sword, because she could hear nothing over it, either.

She reached for the door to silence the screech, then thought better of it and withdrew her hand. If someone had broken into the trailer and that person was still inside, she would give away her presence by securing the door.

But just as the thought flickered through her mind, two things happened in quick succession:

First, Kate noticed with sudden alarm that a circle had been sliced out of the door's screen, giving access to the latch. Then, out of her peripheral vision, she caught a blur of motion off her left side. Black clothing, barely visible in the darkness of night.

She tried to duck away but there was nowhere to go, and she banged against the side of the trailer as a glancing blow struck the side of her head. She tumbled off the front steps and crashed to the ground, and she knew.

The Beast was here.

29

Kate rolled, moving the instant her body hit the ground, knowing even the slightest hesitation would mean certain death.

A split second later, a heavy *thud* next to her head told her the Beast had leapt off the front landing. A pair of boots materialized in front of her and she swept her arm out laterally, inches above the ground. She hooked an elbow around one ankle and yanked with all the force she could muster, and the Beast stumbled and then fell with a surprised grunt.

Kate searched frantically for her weapon. It had fallen from her hands in the attack, and it had to be here somewhere, it had to be *right here*, but she couldn't find it, and any advantage she might have gained from dropping the much bigger man was vanishing fast.

She gave up on the gun, instead pulling the flashlight from her waistband and wielding it two-handed like a baseball player swinging for the fences. The satisfying *crack* told her she had connected with his skull, but it wasn't enough to stop the Beast. He grunted again and scrambled backward, digging his heels into the yard, flinging dirt and pebbles into Kate's face.

She reached for his boot. Caught it. Felt fingernails ripping off as he kicked harder and dislodged his foot from her grasp.

Then the Beast was up and running, pounding across the weed-strewn front yard toward the cover of the woods, moving much faster than a man his size should be able to.

Kate cursed and sprang to her feet. She sprinted after him, knowing that between his dark clothing and the moonless, overcast night it would be impossible to keep him in her sights if she lost any more ground.

Up ahead, a shadowy figure angled across the yard from the direction of the road, moving fast. The shadow slammed into the big man at full speed, and the jarring impact knocked both figures to the ground.

Kate registered the shadow as Weston and watched him tumble, but she never slowed. His diving tackle had allowed her to close the gap to a few feet.

This was her chance. She pumped her legs and lowered her shoulder and drove toward the Beast's midsection as he was pushing himself to his feet—

—and he was gone.

It was impossible. No one could move that fast.

But somehow he had, and her knockout blow caught only air. Kate crashed into Weston, out of control, and they sprawled apart on the ground. She shoved herself to her feet again, refusing to give up, refusing to accept defeat, and made three more sprinting strides before stepping into a hole in the ground.

Sharp pain shot through her ankle, and she fell again.

And the Beast was gone.

Weston stumbled to her side, breathing heavily. "Are you okay?"

Kate ignored the question and said, "He's heading in the direction of the car. Chris is there alone. Go!"

Weston didn't even take the time to answer. He turned on his heel and began sprinting toward the road and the blind boy who was suddenly on a collision course with a madman.

30

The decision to leave Chris alone in the Rambler had been an easy one for Noah Weston. He'd done it before, comfortable with the notion because Chris was probably the least helpless blind kid on the planet. He had suspected strongly that Kate would need his help, and he had been right.

But now he second-guessed himself bitterly as he sprinted along the crumbling Depot Road, risking a broken ankle or worse, dreading what he would find when he rounded the corner and came upon the car, picturing blood and carnage and a young boy lying dead on the side of the road.

The Rambler came into view, still parked on the sandy shoulder, and Weston feared the worst. The rear passenger door hung open, weak yellow light illuminating the apparently empty interior. He rushed to the car, knowing the Beast could still be here waiting to ambush him but not caring.

Nothing mattered but checking on Chris.

The car was empty.

He walked around it, sweeping his eyes left to right, from the side of the vehicle to the tree line. Knelt and peered under the car, knowing he would see nothing in the darkness but doing it anyway.

"Damn it," he muttered. "The bastard took him, and it's my fault, and now—"

I'm here.

"Where? Where's 'here?' Are you okay?"

I'm fine. I felt him coming and hid in the woods.

"Which side of the car are you on? I'll come and get you."

There was no answer and Weston turned toward the tree line

and there Chris was. He stood on the side of the road, his sightless eyes trained on Weston's exact position. It was unexpected, creepy, and the best thing he had ever seen.

"Let's go," he said, hustling the boy into the car. "The Beast could be anywhere and we're out here like sitting ducks."

He's gone. I can still feel him, but he's not close like he was before.

"Are you sure?"

He didn't even slow down to check out the car, he just kept going. He must have been parked somewhere off the side of the road. I don't think he'll come back tonight.

"If he does, I'll kick his head in."

Weston's phone vibrated.

He glanced at the caller ID. Kate. No surprise there; who else would it be?

"I found Chris," he said into the phone without preamble. "He's fine. He felt the Beast coming and hid. We must have really shaken the bastard, because he passed the Rambler right on by. Chris says he didn't even slow down to check it out."

"Not much of a victory," Kate said. "He should be in custody or dead right now."

"And one or more of *us* could just as easily have wound up dead. Hang on for a minute. I'm gonna make sure Chris is all set and then I'll be back to help you."

"No," Kate said. "Chris was terrified the last time he came this close to the Beast. We're lucky he didn't tune out tonight like he did back at The Mission. Stay there, just in case the fucker changes his mind and comes back.

"Chris says he isn't coming back."

"And Chris has been wrong before. It's not worth the risk. I'm gonna check out the house and be back in a few."

The call clicked off and Weston stuffed the phone into his pocket. He thought about hiking back to the Melanson house anyway; it wasn't as if he hadn't disregarded Kate's wishes before.

Then he sighed and climbed into the car. The Beast was gone. Kate was a professional. She could handle the situation at Dani's house, whatever it was.

And she was right about one thing.

If he left and the Beast returned, it was unlikely that Christopher would manage to cheat death again.

31

Chris was okay, and that was a wonderful thing. But the relief Kate felt was tempered by her concern about what she would find inside the Melansons' trailer. The Beast's presence here meant the situation was bad.

Probably very bad.

And while she had no idea how he had learned of their relationship to Dani Melanson, there was absolutely no doubt in her mind it was what had brought him to their door.

The wind had begun to pick up again and now it howled and moaned in the trees. She limped across the yard toward the trailer's front steps, testing her Maglite as she went. The metal was crumpled and the lens cover cracked, but the flashlight beam still worked, and she swept it back and forth, looking for her gun.

A dull glint caught her eye as she approached the stairs. The Beretta had dropped onto the bottom step, and she picked it up, relieved to have it back in her possession.

She held on to the weapon as she stepped to the front door. The Beast was gone but she wasn't about to put it away.

She took a deep breath, steeling her nerves.

Then she slipped through the doorway and into hell.

The light Kate had seen spilling weakly out the kitchen window wasn't much brighter inside the trailer, but it provided more than enough illumination to reveal that a terrible struggle had taken place.

An end table had been overturned. A cut glass lamp lay shattered on the floor next to it. The couch Mrs. Melanson had been sitting on yesterday had been jarred out of position, jutting into the small living room at an odd angle. Cushions were scattered across the room. Playing cards littered the floor.

And blood was everywhere. Even in the dim light, Kate could see splatters and pools that were only just beginning to congeal around their edges. She knew the Beast was gone but she wasn't about to ignore her law enforcement experience, and that experience told her she had to clear the trailer, ensure the home invader really was gone, and find the source of all the blood.

She knew what she was about to discover but pushed the possibility to the back of her mind. She would not acknowledge its reality until she saw it with her own two eyes.

The front door opened into approximately the middle of the trailer, but clearing this portion of the home was easy. The area to Kate's right was wide open, consisting only of the living room where the bloody struggle seemed to have taken place. She crossed it in a half-dozen steps, moving carefully to avoid the blood, and in seconds had cleared a small closet.

She then turned and crossed the room again, this time moving to a short hallway running along the rear of the trailer behind the kitchen. Two doors lined the hallway, both on the right side, both closed.

Kate took a deep breath, exhaling slowly, and then eased the first of the doors open, slipping back against the wall as she did. She waited a heartbeat and then eased around the now-open door, leading with her gun, scanning the room quickly. It was a bedroom, and she could see immediately that there was nowhere for anyone to hide. Two closets took up the right side of the room, but their doors had been removed and it was clear no one was lurking inside either of them.

The double bed in the middle of the room was nothing more than a box spring placed directly on the floor and topped by a mattress. There was no way anyone could be hiding under it. On top of the bed were the obscenely naked bodies of Dani Melanson's parents. They lay side-by-side, their sightless eyes open and fixed on the ceiling.

Kate's sense of dread intensified as she checked each of the victims for a pulse. She had no doubt they were already dead, it was obvious, and she should finish clearing the house before doing anything else, but she checked anyway.

She was right. They were gone.

She stepped back and took in the scene. At least one, if not both, of the Melansons had been killed in the living area—all that blood hadn't gotten out there by itself—and then dragged into the bedroom and hurriedly staged on the bed.

There was nothing she could do for either of these victims. She slipped out of the bedroom and moved to the second door, dreading what she would find when she opened it.

She was sweating, feeling sick. The air inside the trailer was rancid, thick with the smell of blood and sweat and death, and Kate's stomach was doing slow rolls, threatening to make her lose her dinner just as Christopher had a little while ago.

She swallowed heavily and turned the knob.

Pushed the door open with her foot, again taking cover against the wall.

Stepped into the room and gasped, staggering backward into the doorframe. Her eyes widened in shock and horror at the sight of Dani Melanson's corpse.

The girl's body was slumped over a small desk in the corner of the room, dressed in a cotton nightgown that at one time had been covered in a floral pattern but was now covered in her blood. It had soaked completely through the material at her stomach and chest, where the majority of the damage had been done with the attacker's blade. A desk lamp had been lit, bathing the girl in awful yellow light.

Kate crossed the room, unconcerned any longer with stealth, or with protecting herself against a potential assailant, or with anything besides checking for signs of life she knew already she would not find. The amount of blood soaking into Dani's bed told Kate the girl had been attacked while sleeping, killed and then dragged to the desk, where she had been posed with her head resting on her right arm.

Kate placed two fingers against the side of Dani's neck, just under her left ear. Her skin in that area was coated in blood that had leaked out of her mouth. Kate did her best to ignore the significance of that fact. It was too horrible to contemplate. Her fingers were shaking so badly they slipped in the blood and she knew that even if there were a pulse, she would never feel it unless she got herself under control.

So she forced herself to slow down. Take a deep breath. Try again.

But there was nothing. No sign of life. She could press her fingers to this poor girl's neck until hell froze over and she wouldn't be rewarded with a pulse.

Dani was dead.

Murdered along with her parents by the Beast.

And Christopher had known about it, somehow, even though he was fast asleep and miles away at the time of the attack.

He had known.

Kate felt faint. Her head was spinning. She was in danger of hyperventilating. She had investigated dozens of similar crimes in her career, visited plenty of similar crime scenes. Some had been worse than this, if assigning a value to the horror was even possible.

But this atrocity, perpetrated on an innocent child who reminded Kate so much of a thirteen-year-old version of herself, was emotionally and mentally staggering. Dani Melanson had made her reluctance to return home crystal clear, and she had been forced to do exactly that by Kate and Weston.

And now she was dead, murdered in spectacularly brutal fashion and then posed with her head on her desk like a student who had fallen asleep studying.

It was a punch in the gut, followed by an uppercut to the jaw and then a kick in the shins. Bile rushed up Kate's gullet and she choked it back, and as she did, she choked back a sob, too.

And she knew the horror wasn't over yet.

Because blood had flowed out of Dani's mouth and down her neck.

A lot of blood.

Which could mean only one thing.

Kate picked a pencil up off the desk and placed it between the dead girl's teeth, using it as a lever to gently pry her mouth open.

She knew what she would see before ever picking up the

pencil, but she had a role to play.

Dani Melanson was an innocent pawn, one who had contributed her life to this obscene tableau. The least Kate could do was to play her own part out to the end, even if she already knew what that end held in store.

She pulled the flashlight out of the waistband of her jeans with her left hand as she held the pencil in her right.

Flicked it on and shone the beam into Dani's mouth.

And closed her eyes, sinking to her knees in guilt and shame and despair.

Dani's tongue was gone.

32

The walk from the trailer to the Rambler seemed to take forever, despite the fact that Weston had driven to the end of the Melanson driveway while Kate was inside the trailer. The skies had opened up, and the gusty wind whipped the raindrops sideways, stinging her face and soaking her to the bone in a matter of minutes.

And she was heartbroken. Kate had seen more death than most people would face in ten lifetimes, much of it violent and disheartening. But with the possible exception of her mother's murder, not a single case had affected her as deeply as this one.

She trudged along the side of the weedy dirt driveway, head down, trying to process what she'd seen. The Beast had slaughtered a family—including an innocent young girl—for no other reason than to make a statement. Having now made it, she was certain he would be satisfied to allow Weston and Kate to wallow in their failings.

He would insist on it, in fact. The Beast that Kate had come to know and loathe was not about to go to the trouble of executing this brutally effective plan, only to eliminate the very witnesses for whom he had orchestrated it.

If tattooing the children at The Mission was meant to drive home his superiority over his pursuers, the killing of Dani and her family, Kate knew, was his twisted exclamation point, the icing on his cake of psychosis. Somehow he had learned—perhaps through his own intuition, perhaps some other way—of the girl's involvement with Kate and Weston, and had used that knowledge in the most brutally effective manner.

Dani was dead and it was Kate's fault.

She realized she was shivering violently and didn't care. The howling wind and the central Maine night made the rain feel like tendrils of ice dripping under her collar and rolling down her skin, chilling her to the bone.

Or perhaps that chill was radiating outward from her soul; perhaps she would never feel warm or comfortable again.

Maybe she didn't want to. She certainly didn't deserve to.

She was looking down, lost in her thoughts, when she damned near walked right into the Rambler's front grill. She stepped to the side and opened the front door as the headlights flashed on and the engine rumbled to life.

She dropped heavily onto the front seat, physically and mentally exhausted. Rainwater streamed from her soaked clothing onto the seat and floor of Weston's car.

She didn't care about that either.

When Kate's drenched form materialized out of the storm directly in front of the Rambler, Weston breathed such a loud sigh of relief he was a little surprised he didn't wake Chris, who had fallen into an uneasy slumber.

Kate fell into the passenger seat next to him, dropping her head into her hands even before closing the door. The wind whipped through the car, bringing with it icy raindrops.

"Jesus," Weston said. "You're soaked. And what took you so long? We were..." His voice trailed away as he got a good look at her. She reached out and pulled her door closed.

"You look like hell," he said gently. "Was it as bad as I think it was?"

"They're all dead," she whispered. "Murdered in their trailer. And Dani's tongue was missing."

Weston stared at her for what felt like a very long time.

"Jesus," he said once he found his voice. "And her parents? Did he take their tongues, too?"

Kate shook her head. "Only Dani."

And Christopher knew, Weston thought. He couldn't decipher what was happening, but he knew. Then the significance of Kate's last statement struck home like a hammer to the side of the head.

He didn't want to say what he was thinking, but realized there was no reason to leave it unspoken. Kate was far too intelligent and quick-witted not to have thought of it herself. "So it was another message to us."

She nodded in the darkness next to him. He couldn't see her do it, but he knew, nevertheless.

"Three more people are dead," she said dully. "Including one beautiful, innocent young girl, and it's our fault. It's directly and unequivocally our fault." Her voice hitched on the last word and Weston realized she was sobbing quietly.

"Kate," he said. "It's nobody's fault but his."

"We should have kept her with us. She didn't want to go home, we should have let her stay with us and—"

"And what?" He spoke as gently as he could but knew he had to quell her line of reasoning. "She had a family, Kate. Legal guardians. We had no lawful standing to keep her with us, and there is absolutely no reason to believe that if we had brought her home tomorrow, or the next day, or even next week or next month, things would have turned out any differently. We already knew the Beast was brutal and relentless. He wasn't about to stop until he got what he wanted, which in this case was Dani Melanson and her family dead."

"And a point made to us."

"Yes," he agreed. "And a point made to us."

"How do we tell Christopher? He'll be heartbroken."

You don't have to tell me anything. I'm awake.

His voice inside Weston's head was calm and reasoned, in marked contrast to the fear and desperation he had displayed earlier.

Kate turned in her seat. "I'm so sorry, Chris. I should have—"

No, Kate. There was nothing you could have done. There was nothing any of us could have done.

"The authorities will be looking for us," Weston said.

"Why? There's nothing to tie us to those poor people."

"You must have left fingerprints, footprints, other forensic evidence when you went through that trailer."

"Maybe. Maybe not. I wore gloves and wiped down the door latch, so there won't be any fingerprints. And even though there was a lot of blood splatter..." She paused. "I'm sorry, Chris. You didn't need to hear that. I wasn't thinking."

It's okay, Kate. This sort of thing isn't exactly new to me.

She sighed. "Even though there was a lot of blood splatter inside the home, I was very careful not to step in any of it and leave tracks. Now, there may be footprints outside the trailer—it's wet and muddy out there—but, again, I was very careful. The greatest likelihood is of them finding a hair. The wind was gusting pretty violently, especially as I exited the trailer. It's possible I left that type of evidence, but I don't really think so. I had my cap on the entire time.

"In any event," she continued after a short silence, "there's nothing I can do about it now. But we do have to inform the police as soon as possible."

"So we buy a new burner," Weston said. "We can drop an anonymous tip as soon as we put a little distance between ourselves and the crime scene. The question is..."

"What do we do now?"

"Yes. We came to Maine to get a line on this bastard, but I'd say this trip can reasonably be classified as a total disaster. Three more people are dead in addition to Peter LeBlanc—"

"At least," Kate interjected. "There may be others we don't know about yet. Your concern about Hamilton may have been warranted."

"True," Weston conceded. "At least three more people are dead, all because we took the Beast's bait in the first place. And we're no closer to tracking him down now than we were five days ago. We have no idea where he's gone, or even if he's left Brunswick."

"That's not entirely true," Kate said softly. "I have an idea."

"How could you possibly know?"

"Because he told me."

33

Kate felt the heat of Weston's gaze from across the pitch-dark front seat. "He told you where he was going? You two had a nice little chat while you were rolling in the dirt? Is that it?"

"Not exactly. I would have liked nothing better than to put two slugs between his eyes. But he told me, nevertheless."

"I don't suppose you'd care to explain."

She took a deep breath, listening to the reedy sound of the air in her throat. She wondered if she was catching a cold and decided that after tonight it would be a miracle if she didn't. Her head was pounding from stress, and from the blow she had taken from the Beast. And the adrenaline that had fueled her over the last hour or so had suddenly and completely drained from her system, leaving her tired, shaky, and in need of about eighteen hours of sleep.

"I don't know if I should tell you right now," she finally said, thinking of Christopher in the back seat.

Please, Kate. I can handle it. Just say it.

She was too tired to argue, so she didn't.

"The Beast killed Dani in her bed," she said. "But he didn't leave her there. He posed her."

"Posed her how?" Weston asked.

"He placed her in a chair at her desk, with her head resting on her right arm."

"Why would he do that? What's the point?"

"To make sure we received his message."

"What message is that?"

Kate ran a hand over her eyes. She didn't know if she had ever felt this exhausted. "I'll get to that in a minute. After I checked inside her mouth and discovered her tongue had been cut out, I noticed that her right hand was closed around a pen."

She didn't bother to mention the part about dropping onto the floor in despair after seeing the desecration that had been visited upon the girl's mouth. Weston and Chris didn't need to know about her weakness. Nobody needed to know.

"So she was trying to write something when she was killed," Weston said.

"No," Kate told him. "It wasn't like she was holding it with the intention of writing. Her hand had been closed into a fist, and then the pen jammed into it. No one would hold a pen that way naturally or normally."

"Maybe she grabbed it in a panic and tried to use it to defend herself."

"No," Kate said again. "Because there was something else."

"What else?"

"I used a pencil to lever Dani's mouth open. After I discovered her tongue had been removed, I dropped the pencil onto the desk next to her body and tried to regain my composure. It wasn't easy."

"I can imagine," Weston muttered.

"As I stood staring down at the desk, I noticed that the pencil had rolled toward Dani's body, coming to rest next to her hand."

"The hand holding the pen."

"Yes. But its momentum was stopped before reaching her hand, and that didn't make sense. An object in motion, and all that. So I looked more closely at her fist and discovered that underneath it was a slip of paper. I gently lifted Dani's hand and pulled the paper out from under it. There were just a couple of words written on it."

"What words?"

"See for yourself." She reached into the right front pocket of her waterlogged jeans and pulled out a slip of paper.

Weston heard her doing so and said disbelievingly, "You removed evidence from a crime scene? You?"

"I also disturbed a crime scene just by being there. But that's not the point."

"What is, then?"

"The point is that the note was left specifically for us."

Weston took a moment to respond. "What does it say?"

"Turn on the light," she said, and when Weston complied, she flattened the slip of paper between the palms of her hands, smoothing out the wrinkles, and then held it up for his inspection.

The note was maybe four inches wide by four inches high, written on lined paper with ragged edges. It looked as though it had been torn out of a school notebook.

She watched Weston's face as he stared at the paper in the stark light. It was direct communication from the subhuman monster who had taken so much from all of them, and he regarded it the way one might regard a ticking time bomb.

It wouldn't take long to read. The words were large and written in ink. Although the notepaper had become soaked through by the raging storm during Kate's trek back to the Rambler, the writing was still perfectly legible.

Scrawled across the top of the note in what looked like a child's handwriting was:

LUCY <3 MICKEY

And below that, in slightly different color ink, was the word:

FARGO

Weston shook his head and sucked in a breath. "He's taunting us."

"It's what he does," Kate said. "He's gloating, letting us know he's invincible, letting us know that there's nothing we can do to stop him. Telling us he's so unconcerned about our efforts to track him down that he's willing to provide us with advance knowledge of his next destination. Telling us we're no more significant to him than a couple of ants crawling on the floor."

Weston held her eyes for a moment and then looked back down. He gaped at the note, so small and ordinary, and yet so significant.

"Do you think the top line is legit?"

Kate knew he had attempted to phrase the question in a way that Christopher would not understand. If Chris learned the contents of the note, who knew what his reaction would be?

"Looks like it to me," she said.

You don't have to hide it from me. I know what it says.

"How do you...?" Kate's question drifted away. Why ask it when it was unanswerable?

She tried a different tack.

"This note is what this colossal mountain of shit was really all about. A mind-fuck designed by the Beast to demonstrate his superiority over us. Over everyone, but especially over us."

Kate's exhaustion was growing. She wasn't just physically tired, but mentally and emotionally as well. Maybe the Beast really *was* invincible. Maybe he would continue to cut a swath of death and destruction though the United States indefinitely, murdering for sport and disfiguring his victims, and then gloating about it in his own twisted way.

Maybe they really *were* overmatched.

It certainly felt that way.

"So what do we do now?" Weston whispered. His eyes were still locked onto the soaking wet piece of notebook paper, and he sounded as disheartened as Kate felt.

We start driving.

She turned to Chris. "Start driving where?"

North Dakota. Where else?

"Chris, I don't know. That's exactly what he wants. And at least four people are dead because of us."

I know, Kate. I know what we lost. But what's changed? Is there any reason to think the Beast will stop killing if we give up?

"He's right," Weston said to her.

Then we need to leave right now. It's a long way to Fargo, and every minute we sit here second-guessing ourselves is another minute we fall behind.

"But Dani—"

I know, Kate. I know. But we can't allow her death to divert us from what needs to be done. Because that's what he wants. The real reason he's doing this is the opposite of what you think it is.

"What do you mean?"

He's afraid of us, Kate. He's nervous because he knows we're getting closer and closer to shutting him down once and for all.

"Then why not just come after us?"

Sooner or later he will. But not yet. He's a lot like that old man in Michigan. He wants to play games, make us suffer first, because we're giving him a taste of something he's never experienced before.

"And what's that?"

Self-doubt. He doesn't like it. He's afraid of it. This is not the time to stop chasing him. This is the time to turn up the heat. Especially now that we know that Lucy might still be with him.

Kate studied Chris, wondering how a boy this age could be so wise. Could sound so much older than his years. He'd seen a lot in his short life, but was it enough to make her feel as if she were sometimes speaking to an adult?

The thought of that 1995 newspaper article haunted her now. Made her uncertain about everything.

About Chris.

But no matter who or what he was, everything he'd just said made sense. And she needed to trust him.

Weston cleared his throat and turned to the boy. "Maybe he's not going to Fargo at all. Maybe the point of that note is to throw us off his trail. It makes sense, especially if you're right about us making him nervous."

It's not misdirection. He's afraid of us, yes, but he's also trying to convince himself of his invincibility just as much as he's trying to convince us. Maybe more.

It's not misdirection.

He's going to Fargo and so are we.

EPILOGUE

"Continuous, unflagging effort, persistence and determination will win. Let not the man be discouraged who has these."

~James Whitcomb Riley

34

The sun hung suspended over the gunmetal-grey Atlantic as they crossed the Piscataqua River Bridge into New Hampshire, leaving Maine behind them.

For good, Weston hoped.

Christopher was snoring in the back seat, his right arm thrust away from his body, and in the rearview mirror, Weston could see the mysterious circumpunct on the boy's inner wrist. It wasn't showing any signs of fading away and Christopher continued to insist he had no idea where the damned thing had come from.

In front, Kate dozed fitfully next to Weston, her head resting at what looked like an uncomfortable angle against the side window. She seemed to be staying more or less asleep, so he left her alone.

The broadcast signal of the radio station in Portland was beginning to fade away when a solemn-sounding announcer interrupted a forgettable pop tune with a special "breaking news" bulletin.

Weston reached for the dial, impatient with the reception and anxious to find a better station, when the fuzzy, staticky voice of the newscaster caught his attention.

"We interrupt our broadcast to bring you news of a horrific series of murders up the coast in Brunswick."

Weston jerked his hand off the radio knob as if it burned and leaned forward in an attempt to catch the man's words, which were now fading in and out as the Rambler sped toward Interstate 90 and the long trek west to North Dakota.

"Conspiracy theories are flying this morning with the discovery of the body of Brunswick resident Jane Hamilton, found murdered in her home overnight. Police are releasing few specifics at this hour, but a source close to the investigation did tell WPWM News, on condition of anonymity, that the deceased woman's body was mutilated in some unspecified manner.

"Hamilton, longtime director of the Maine Home for Children with Special Needs, known locally as 'The Mission,' is the third person connected with the facility to be killed in the last five days. She joins counselor Peter LeBlanc, murdered outside the grounds of The Mission last week, and thirteen-year-old Dani Melanson, sister of a young Mission resident, who was killed along with her parents in a separate incident overnight inside their Lisbon home.

"What role the Maine Home for Children with Special Needs may have played in the murders is unknown at this time. However, a massive investigation is being launched, one involving not just the Brunswick Police, but also the Maine State Police and the Maine Department of Health and Human Services, which oversees the group home. Rumors of FBI involvement in the investigation have not been confirmed, but neither have they been ruled out.

"A press conference has been scheduled for eleven a.m. at Brunswick Police Headquarters. Stay tuned to WPWM as we carry the press conference live, and for immediate updates to this explosive story as they happen. We now return you..."

The signal dissolved into a jumble of static and interference, and Weston switched off the radio. He had heard enough.

He drove in silence for a long time, watching the broken white lines of the interstate flash beneath the Rambler, thinking about psychosis and obsession and death.

He felt no sense of triumph that his instincts about Hamilton had turned out to be true, and he knew she had likely been long dead by the time he had managed to break though the Beast's mind block. To remember what had been said.

The bastard was more powerful than Weston would ever have believed.

But he believed it now.

He did feel some relief, however, that Livvie Barnstead had apparently escaped death. Her lack of inclusion in the news report would seem to indicate she had lucked out.

So that was one out of six, if you didn't count the kids. One out of six who had survived this latest rampage.

Not much of a victory, as Kate had said, and he figured he'd wait awhile before he told her about Hamilton.

If he ever told her at all.

She stirred quietly, lifted her head off the window, blinked a couple of times. Ran her tongue across her teeth and grimaced.

"You must be exhausted," she said.

"I'm fine."

"What time is it?"

"Seven-thirty a.m."

"Want me to drive for a while so you can rest?"

"I'm good. Thanks."

Kate stared at him a little longer. He could see out of the corner of his eye that she was gazing at him levelly. Then she eased her head down and went back to sleep.

By the time she awoke again, they were an hour closer to Fargo.

Other books in the *Linger* series available for purchase now

We hope you enjoyed this book, and if you did, we'd greatly appreciate a quick review on Amazon, Goodreads and other review sites. And be sure to tell your friends about the book as well.

Authors and publishing houses live and die by our readers, and reviews go a long way toward spreading the word about a good book.

If you have any questions about the Linger Series or any of our other books, feel free to contact us at *BraunHausMedia.com* and sign up for our newsletter.

Thank you.

Robert Gregory Browne
Creative Director
Braun Haus Media, LLC